"What a—————————————————
Jake dema—————————

Even in t—————————————
color blosso———————————— a moment of
regret that he d embarrassed her, but she provoked him. If he had to get her mad in order to
understand her—

"I'm not hiding anything," Libby insisted. She
moved to leave, but he grabbed her wrist and held
her there.

"You've got a body that doesn't quit, and you're
hiding it under a thousand yards of fabric. You've
got a couple of feet of what I suspect is hair like silk
knotted up so tight you're giving yourself head-
aches. You wear men's glasses that conceal most of
your face, but they can't hide those blue ponds
you've got for eyes. Why?" he demanded.

Her patience gone, Libby jerked free of him, but
she didn't run. Only cowards ran from a confrontation, and she wasn't a coward.

Before she could speak, he ran his finger down
her cheek and felt the shock that held her immobile, the warmth just beneath the surface. When
he pressed his fingertips to the throbbing evidence
of her hidden passion and obvious fury, he saw her
eyes widen with surprise and heard what he hoped
was a muted cry of desire. Her scent of honeysuckle seduced him anew.

"You're hiding, Libby, even if only from yourself,"
he insisted.

She found her voice finally. "You are thoroughly
tactless, Mr. Stratton, and remarkably rude."

He laughed, and mentally applauded her spirit.
He savored the fire blazing in her huge eyes, and
he loved the idea of stoking that fire until it
produced an inferno capable of engulfing them
both. . . .

WHAT ARE *LOVESWEPT* ROMANCES?

They are stories of true romance and touching emotion. We believe those two very important ingredients are constants in our highly sensual and very believable stories in the *LOVESWEPT* line. Our goal is to give you, the reader, stories of consistently high quality that may sometimes make you laugh, sometimes make you cry, but are always fresh and creative and contain many delightful surprises within their pages.

Most romance fans read an enormous number of books. Those they truly love, they keep. Others may be traded with friends and soon forgotten. We hope that each *LOVESWEPT* romance will be a treasure—a "keeper." We will always try to publish

LOVE STORIES YOU'LL NEVER FORGET
BY AUTHORS YOU'LL ALWAYS REMEMBER

The Editors

Loveswept 502

Laura Taylor
Starfire

BANTAM BOOKS
NEW YORK · TORONTO · LONDON · SYDNEY · AUCKLAND

STARFIRE

A Bantam Book / October 1991

If you would be interested in receiving protective vinyl
covers for your Loveswept books, please write to this address
for information:

Loveswept
Bantam Books
P.O. Box 985
Hicksville, NY 11802

ISBN 0-553-44167-1

Published simultaneously in the United States and Canada

Bantam Books are published by Bantam Books, a division
of Bantam Doubleday Dell Publishing Group, Inc. Its trademark, consisting of the words "Bantam Books" and the
portrayal of a rooster, is Registered in U.S. Patent and
Trademark Office and in other countries. Marca Registrada.
Bantam Books, 666 Fifth Avenue, New York, New York
10103.

PRINTED IN THE UNITED STATES OF AMERICA

OPM   0 9 8 7 6 5 4 3 2 1

One

Associate Professor Libby Kincaid felt her heart plummet right down to her kneecaps. "You want *me* to act as liaison for Jake Stratton during his six-week lecture series?" she clarified, her soft voice even more subdued than usual.

Unable to believe her ears, she glanced from the somewhat pudgy dean of Hancock College, Bill Cassidy, to Avery Mendenhall, the austere-looking chairman of the business department. Libby managed to conceal the dismay she felt as she studied the two men. Under more pleasant circumstances, they often reminded her of Mutt and Jeff. At the moment, however, they resembled an uneven roadblock.

Avery Mendenhall reluctantly admitted, "I realize that I promised you a reprieve from liaison work this semester, Libby, but I'm afraid I'm going to have to ask for your cooperation. You're simply the best person for this particular assignment."

"But why?" she asked before she could stop herself.

Avery looked decidedly uncomfortable, but Libby suddenly didn't care about his discomfort. Nor did she care about, or for, the speculative look on Dean Cassidy's face. Her mind was too occupied with the chaos these two were about to set into motion in her life.

Libby, who thrived on order and harmony, had already planned every minute of the coming semester. Having the schedule she'd created tampered with meant that she would spend the next few months scrambling to make her textbook deadline.

Although tempted to let out a howl of utter frustration, she groaned silently instead. She also held on to her temper and maintained the image of restraint and control she took pride in projecting to the world.

"Why?" she asked a second time.

"Quite frankly, our decision is based equally on the fact that you aren't falling all over yourself to get the job—unlike most of the department staff—and on your successful track record working liaison. Jake Stratton isn't exactly our typical guest lecturer, is he?"

"No, Avery, he's not," Libby conceded grudgingly.

She didn't know Jake Stratton, of course, but his name had been on the tip of every tongue since the announcement of his lecture series the previous week.

Mature women, colleagues one and all, giggled every time his name came up in conversation. The men waxed poetic about his entrepreneurial skills and the women he dated. And nearly every student in the business department discussed his most recent book, *Ethics in the Workplace*, in hushed, reverent whispers. Libby thought they'd all lost their minds.

Summoning her wits, she opted for a calm presentation of her case. "My schedule is *very* tight this semester. I have my regular class load, half of Stan Turner's classes while he's away on sabbatical, student-counseling responsibilities, and a textbook deadline."

When neither man said anything, she decided to cut to the proverbial chase. She betrayed her nervousness briefly when she fingered the bun at her nape. Anchored so securely that it routinely produced a headache by the end of the day, the snug knot restrained a waist-length silken fall of dark hair.

"Would it be possible for me to exchange liaison assignments with another staff member for a time period later in the semester? I'm quite overextended as it is," she finished with characteristic quiet dignity and formal manner.

Libby lowered her hands to her lap, her fingers meshing together in a clenched tangle. She held very still as she waited, and she breathed a silent prayer. The tension suffusing her slender body tightened her muscles until they ached, but she didn't stir.

Instead, she watched Avery Mendenhall and Bill Cassidy glance at each other. She noted their surprise, and she sensed their reluctance to honor her request, but she knew she wouldn't be able to live with herself if she didn't at least try to protect the limited time she had left to complete the manuscript for her first textbook.

"I'm sorry, Libby, but the schedule stands. I know there are several teachers on staff who would dearly love to relieve you of this assignment, but I'm convinced that you're the best candidate for the job. Good organization on your part will of course be a must, but Dean Cassidy and I are confident that you can handle Mr. Stratton for six short weeks and still fulfill your other obligations."

Libby nodded, but she still couldn't dismiss the inner panic she felt. Publish or perish. It was both a challenge and a crucible for anyone seeking advancement in the academic ranks. In her case it was also a meaningful step toward satisfying her deep-seated craving for self-sufficiency and security, both personally and professionally.

Dean Cassidy abandoned his role as an observer and suggested, "You can always request a deadline extension from your publisher, Professor Kincaid."

Stubborn determination flared to life inside her, strengthening her resolve and rekindling an inner fire that brought a rush of color to her pale cheeks. "I can't do that, sir. I've made a commitment, and I intend to honor it."

"Are you acquainted with Jake Stratton?" he asked.

Libby's blue eyes widened in surprise. "Of course not, Dean Cassidy. We don't exactly travel in the same social circles."

"Then you have no personal objections to working with him?"

Libby shifted uncomfortably in her chair, but she longed to say, "Look at me. I'm plain. I can't make small talk to save my life. I rarely socialize."

Instead of speaking, Libby remained quiet for several moments. Her pride wouldn't allow her to admit how insecure she felt at the prospect of trying to cope with a man who lunched regularly at the White House, jetted around the world on a weekly basis, and dated starlets, making him the envy of most of the world's male population.

Instead of pointing out the obvious, Libby resigned herself to the inevitable. "I have no personal objections whatsoever, Dean Cassidy."

"Excellent. Now, I'd advise you to make good use of your time until Jake's arrival on the fifteenth, Professor Kincaid. The man's a workaholic, so he'll keep you very busy while he's here."

Libby stood and smoothed the skirt of her calf-length brown jumper before collecting her purse and briefcase. "Thank you for your confidence in me. I'll do my very best to accommodate Mr. Stratton's scheduling needs."

"Just make him feel welcome, Professor Kincaid, and give him the benefit of your experience as a teacher as you guide him through the lecture series. Jake's been a generous friend to Hancock since he left here seventeen years ago, and I want him treated with courtesy and respect."

The dean hesitated. Libby sensed that he was weighing his words carefully. She couldn't help wondering why.

"Jake Stratton is a highly ethical and intelligent man. Even more important, he cares about people and the quality of their lives. The fact that he has the respect of the international business community and the confidence of several world leaders should tell you a great deal about him already. And although he lives a very visible and well-documented life, thanks to the press, he isn't your typical celebrity. In short, Professor Kincaid, I think he'll surprise you."

Libby barely managed to keep from frowning. She didn't like surprises, but she kept that piece of information to herself. Jake Stratton might be the most accomplished man on the planet—Dean Cassidy obviously thought he was—but he was still going to disrupt her life in a major way.

She wished both men a pleasant afternoon and left the conference room, her thoughts on the task ahead of her. When she paused in the hallway to adjust the strap of her shoulder bag, she heard a portion of the conversation that followed.

"Jake'll be good for her," Dean Cassidy observed. "He might even manage to loosen her up a little."

"Her students love her, Bill, despite her rather formal manner."

"I know that. And I've never questioned her dedication, but I've always wondered why she feels the need to remain so aloof and look so drab. Surely she could do something about that wardrobe of hers."

Avery chuckled. "Well, at least we won't have to worry about her trying to seduce the illustrious Jake Stratton while he's here. I was quite amazed by the hungry gleam in the eyes of some of the women in my department when they learned he was scheduled to conduct a lecture series. Fortunately Libby seems singularly unimpressed by the man and his reputation."

Their laughter nudged a stunned Libby from her

frozen pose just outside the partially open door of the conference room. Embarrassed to be the object of their humor, although the image she projected was of her own making, she forced herself to take deep, calming breaths as she made her way down a long hallway and out of the administration building.

A gust of unseasonably cold wind hit her in the face like a slamming door when she stepped outside. Another series of gusts tugged at the errant tendrils of dark hair framing her heart-shaped face, heightened the glow of her flawless complexion, and flattened the loose fabric of her jumper against her long-limbed and surprisingly shapely figure.

With her head bowed and her briefcase clutched tightly against her chest, Libby tried to blame the tears stinging her large, thickly lashed blue eyes on the blustery fall weather, but she failed miserably. Feeling unexpectedly vulnerable and alone, she couldn't stop the memories of her past that surged into her mind as she hurried along the winding, tree-lined path that linked the Hancock College administration buildings to one of several campus parking lots.

She realized that she would never completely escape the reality that she was the unwanted product of the marriage of an alcoholic rodeo roustabout and his weak-willed wife. She would never forget the unwelcome attention of shiftless men similar to her father during her adolescence, men who had provoked fear in her innocent heart and prompted her to conceal her physical attributes. Nor could she dismiss her apprehension that someone might discover the truth about her past.

Libby stopped short when she stepped into a patch of sunlight at the end of the path. With considerable effort she put aside her hurt that the dean of the college and her immediate superior both considered her dowdy enough to handle their prize lecturer. She suddenly realized that the choice of succeeding or failing to achieve the goals she'd set for herself remained in her hands, just as they had fourteen years ago when, at the age of sixteen, she had fled the nomadic and unstable existence of the rodeo circuit.

She could, she reasoned further, allow herself to be victimized by an unwanted liaison assignment, just as she'd been victimized by her parents' alcoholism during her childhood. Or she could remain focused on her dream of security via tenure and a full professorship at Hancock College.

An instinctive unwillingness to be victimized had saved her once before. Older and far wiser now, Libby sensed that it could save her again.

She would do her duty, but no one, she vowed silently as she unlocked the door to her car, would be permitted to keep her from remaining in control of her life and her future. Not Dean Cassidy. Not Professor Avery Mendenhall. And certainly not Mr. Jake Stratton.

Three weeks and two days following her conversation with Bill Cassidy and Avery Mendenhall, a subdued Libby Kincaid found the only quiet corner in Dean Cassidy's home and took a moment to collect herself.

The welcome party for Jake Stratton was in full swing, with nearly every department chairman, professor, and associate professor at Hancock College, plus assorted spouses, in attendance when she'd arrived a few minutes earlier. With no time to change following her last class, Libby still wore her standard campus uniform of flat-heeled shoes and a calf-length gray jumper with long sleeves and a lace collar.

Libby sipped a soft drink and watched Jake Stratton work the crowded room with the ease of a savvy politician. With Dean Cassidy at his side, he exchanged greetings, shook hands, and even posed for an occasional photograph. While she couldn't restrain the cynicism that made her wonder when someone would produce a baby for him to kiss, she also grudgingly acknowledged the charisma of the man.

She never guessed that Jake Stratton disliked being treated like some conquering hero. Instead, she simply assumed that he enjoyed the attention of her peers, who clustered around him like frenzied piranhas at feeding time. Had she been paying attention, Libby would have also realized that the source of her discontent, the man she wished would continue to clutter the pages of supermarket tabloids instead of her life, had already established her quiet alcove as his personal beachhead.

Libby absently noted the predominantly formal attire of those attending the welcome party. Jake Stratton, however, wore snug-fitting denims, a cable-knit sweater that made her think of Ireland, and cowboy boots. She admitted to herself that he was a dynamic package with his dense crop of brown hair, which was longer than she'd expected, his ruddy complexion, intense gray eyes, dramatic dark eyebrows, and a mustache that made him look like a bona fide rake.

There wasn't anything even remotely pretty about him, Libby realized. A rugged, earthy-looking man with a powerful physique, he dwarfed most of the men at the party with his impressive height and the width of his broad shoulders.

Despite her resistance to the idea, she silently conceded that Jake Stratton was probably every woman's secret fantasy. He might have even been hers once upon a time, but she no longer indulged in girlish dreams.

The decibel level of the cocktail party reached a deafening roar during the next ten minutes, as did the brass band performing in Libby's skull. Exhausted by three solid weeks of eighteen-hour workdays, she longed for a quiet meal and a relaxing soak in the tub. Unaware that she was being watched, she closed her eyes on a weary sigh and gently massaged the back of her neck.

"Headache, Professor Kincaid?"

Libby's eyes snapped open. Unprepared for the seductive resonance of Jake Stratton's voice, she straightened abruptly from her slumped position against the alcove wall.

"I've had a long day." As an afterthought, she stuck out her hand. "Welcome to Hancock College, Mr. Stratton."

He took her extended hand, but he didn't release

it even when she politely tried to remove it. "That hairstyle doesn't appear to be helping matters," he observed, his blunt remark and his thorough inspection of her totally in character. "It looks like some form of medieval torture. Maybe you should take out the hairpins."

Libby's eyes blazed a brilliant blue. She jerked her fingers free, discarded the empty cup she held, and closed her hands into tight fists, all her energy focused on trying not to knock his block off.

"My mother had the same problem. The first thing she always did when she got home from work was remove the pins and give her hair a good brushing."

"Thank you for the advice, Mr. Stratton."

"No problem, unless I'm the reason for your headache."

"Do you take credit for everything that happens around you, Mr. Stratton?" she asked, her tone as tart as a sour apple.

His mustache twitched slightly. "I like you, Libby Kincaid. You're not the least bit impressed by me, are you?"

Libby belatedly sensed that a certain decorum on her part might be in order, despite the pounding fury of her headache and nerves that suddenly felt as though they'd been fed through a paper shredder.

"It isn't that I'm not impressed with your credentials," she began, unnerved by the warmth seeping into her body as she looked up at him.

He snapped his fingers, and his eyes sparkled with mischief. "I've got it. You hate social functions that are basically command performances. Me too."

Libby, ever protective of Hancock College, commented, "Dean Cassidy thought this party would be a good way of making you feel welcome. Aren't you enjoying yourself?"

"I don't need the ego stroke, if that's what you mean."

She nodded, although she hardly believed that he didn't secretly savor the adulation.

"What about you?"

She nearly smiled at him. "People rarely stroke my ego. It's not a requirement of mine."

"Mine either." He searched her face for a moment and observed, "You're loyal, too, aren't you? That's good. Bill Cassidy pointed you out to me, by the way. Said people were standing in line to assist me with this lecture series, but I suspect you're one of the few who probably ran for cover, aren't you?"

Gazing away, Libby flushed and nervously pressed her fingertips to her temple. Very few men unsettled her or made her intensely aware of herself as a woman. Jake Stratton, however, masterfully accomplished both jobs in short order. When she looked at him, Libby saw his sudden frown.

"I thought we should get acquainted, but it appears that we need to find you some aspirin first."

"Don't trouble yourself, Mr. Stratton. I'm sure you have more important things to do this evening."

He grinned at the sarcasm that edged her words, and his broad smile nearly blinded her. Libby quickly stepped back a pace. She promptly ran up against solid wall, and felt like a fool.

"Bill Cassidy forgot to tell me you have a temper."

Libby refused to be provoked. "Dean Cassidy doesn't know me well enough to comment on my temperament."

"Still waters run very deep, I see."

"I would've expected someone of your stature to avoid using clichés."

He smiled once again, but Libby was prepared for the impact this time.

"Am I the cause of your headache, Professor Kincaid?" he pressed once again, his voice low and disturbingly intimate.

Libby visibly bristled at his tone, as well as his pursuit of the state of her health. She knew she'd already been far too snappish with him. Unfortunately she ignored the voice in her head that urged her not to let him inspire any further verbal recklessness on her part.

"Don't flatter yourself, Mr. Stratton. What you are is a six-week assignment. Hancock College and our grad students will benefit from your lecture series. Dean Cassidy simply decided to spare you the . . . more eager of my colleagues."

"You didn't want the job."

He appeared unruffled by the possibility, which surprised her given her private conclusions about the probable size of his ego. "No, I did not want the job."

"Not into baby-sitting, I take it."

"That's right, but my personal feelings won't keep me from doing my very best to guide you through the lecture series."

"I'll do *my* very best not to become a burden," he promised, his gray eyes alight with laughter and a disturbing hint of sexual innuendo.

Libby shifted nervously, her normal composure absent as she studied him. Dean Cassidy had been right, she realized. This man was a surprise, and not an altogether unpleasant one. Chagrined by her wayward thoughts and the warmth flowing unchecked through her bloodstream, Libby forced herself to appear unaffected by his unpredictable manner.

"I think we'll work well together, Libby Kincaid, but I am curious about one thing."

"What's that?"

"Are you always so combative?"

She flushed, color staining her cheeks as she glared at him. "Rarely, Mr. Stratton."

"Call me Jake," he suggested. "It's comforting to know I bring out the fire in you."

He towered over her like a tall mountain peak, his wide shoulders blocking her view of the party. Libby experienced a sudden stab of panic. His voice faded to a low roar as he continued to speak. Feeling cut off and cornered in the alcove, Libby took a steadying breath to quell her frantic heart-beat and jostled emotions.

Pure stubbornness, however, prevented her from giving ground and admitting that she needed some space. A memory surfaced in her conscious-ness and reminded her that she'd been trapped once before. It had happened a long time ago, of course, but the memory was vivid and frightening as it flashed through her mind.

Jake couldn't ignore the sudden loss of color in Libby's face. She stiffened when he took a step closer to her, so he immediately moved to one side of the alcove. "Are you claustrophobic?"

She didn't answer. She couldn't answer. Instead, she looked up at him, her eyes bottomless pools of blue, her flawless skin nearly translucent. The memory of being trapped and crudely handled by a hard-drinking cowboy during her adolescence slowly faded.

"Are you all right, Libby?"

She felt the probing force of his narrow-eyed gaze. Angry with herself for revealing a secret vulnerability, she decided she'd had enough. "I'm fine, but I do have to excuse myself now, Mr. Stratton." All business once again, Libby briskly told him, "I left a folder with some basic lesson plans for you with the concierge at your hotel. We'll go over your agenda when I collect you in the morning at eight-fifteen." She gave him a dismissive smile. "I hope you enjoy the rest of your evening."

Jake grinned at her. Her defenses in disarray, Libby felt the sizzle and burn of his smile right down to her toes. The realization that she wasn't immune to him infused her with the energy she needed to be on her way.

Intent on getting as far from Jake Stratton as possible, Libby tried to dart past him. She didn't see the waiter approaching from the opposite end of the hallway. She squeaked in protest when she felt a large hand settle on her left shoulder and an arm slide around her waist.

Jake made short work of pulling her out of

harm's way. He jerked her back against his chest as the waiter raced by, a tray of filled champagne goblets awkwardly positioned above his head.

Libby appreciated Jake's intervention. What she didn't appreciate was being indebted to him.

Two

Libby didn't understand why Jake seemed reluctant to release her. As her shock slowly drained away, she became increasingly aware of the lean, hard strength of the man with whom she would spend much of the next six weeks.

With her back pressed firmly against his broad chest, she trembled as she absorbed the heat emanating from his powerful body and felt the accelerated thudding of his heart. She shifted forward, but the tightening of his arms brought her into stunning contact with his narrow hips and the suggestive reality of his maleness.

Tensing, she caught her lower lip between her teeth. His possessive embrace induced a flood of uncertainty. Awareness sizzled along her nerve endings like tiny droplets of water on a hot griddle. The pulse points in her body hammered wildly. Even as she stilled the cry of disbelief welling inside her, Libby struggled to project a calm she didn't feel.

She reminded herself to breathe. When she did, the subtle, sensual scent of Jake's after-shave filled her senses. She froze when his chin settled atop her head. He exhaled heavily, the sound oddly ragged to Libby's ears.

She experienced a unique emotion, an emotion so foreign that she didn't even want to acknowledge it. That she could feel safe, even secure, in the arms of a man she didn't know thoroughly unnerved and bewildered her.

Shaken by the protective quality of his embrace, Libby forced herself out of his arms. She turned slowly and looked up at him, her blue eyes enormous with surprise and confusion. She felt a moment of stark vulnerability as his gaze swept across her pale face.

He reached out. Her eyes widened, and her pulse thrummed and vibrated. He let his hand fall back to his side, his expression puzzled. They stared at each other until a burst of laughter exploded nearby and jerked them both back to the present.

Awkwardness, a renewed rush of tension, and a myriad of other conflicting emotions nearly swamped her. She retreated behind a facade of exacting formality. Extending her hand, she said, "Thank you for your assistance, Mr. Stratton."

He ignored her courteous gesture and ground out, "Jake."

Libby almost flinched, but she caught herself before she reacted to his sharp command. She pressed damp palms to her sides. "Thank you, Jake," she repeated, saying his name far more gently than she intended. "I'll see you in the morning."

He frowned as she began to turn away. "I'll drive you home, Libby."

She paused, reluctance and unexpected pleasure mingling inside her. "There's no need to inconvenience yourself. It's only a few blocks from here, and I really prefer to walk."

"There's every need. Besides, I could use some fresh air."

"It's early yet," she reminded him, her tone of voice and her manner growing increasingly wary as she struggled to contain her response to him. "I'm sure you don't want to disappoint Dean Cassidy and his wife."

Jake glanced at his watch. "I was in London the last time I got out of bed, so my day's been longer than you can imagine. Bill and Miriam will understand."

Unwilling to debate the issue, Libby simply nodded. "I have to find my coat and purse." She slipped away without another word, certain she would be unlocking her front door long before he even noticed her absence.

Jake watched her cross the hallway and lose herself in the crush of people gathered in the Cassidys' spacious living room. Her intent was obvious, but he said nothing. Instead, he went in search of his host and hostess as he pondered Libby Kincaid and his startling response to her.

Jake thanked the Cassidys for their hospitality, retrieved his jacket, and made his way outside. As he stood at the end of the flagstone path in front of the brick home, he breathed deeply of the crisp night air and considered how unexpectedly right Libby Kincaid had felt in his arms, though she seemed compelled to confront the world with all the style of a mudhen.

He also recalled the faint honeysuckle fragrance of her hair, and he savored the thought of just how satisfying it would be to see her long hair released from bondage and streaming down her back. Her naked back. He nearly groaned at the vividness of the image that flashed into his mind.

Desire stalked him, surprising him with its intensity and reminding him of the utter lushness of her breasts, the narrowness of her waist, and the tantalizingly feminine welcome inherent in the cradling shape of her hips. Slim and toned, her body taunted and seduced him, despite the fact that she insisted on concealing it beneath several yards of shapeless fabric.

What's she hiding from? he wondered. *And why?*

Jake didn't like the reasons that occurred to him. He loathed the possibility that someone might have hurt her once or forced her to do something that she hadn't wanted.

Instinct told him that she had been as startled as he by the combustible quality of their brief physical contact. Experience suggested that she, too, had felt the chemistry that had leapt to life between them.

Jake heard the Cassidys' front door open and close and the footsteps that immediately followed while he recalled once again the searing sense of loss he'd felt when Libby had fled his arms. She wasn't at all like the women he knew. Her blatant indifference to him, her apparent preoccupation with her own agenda, even her obvious lack of experience with men, provoked an array of diverse emotions in him.

Jake, secure enough to know that he rarely inspired indifference in any woman, experienced an unexpected flash of pleasure that Libby Kincaid wasn't the kind of woman who needed a man. He smiled, instinctively challenged by the fact that she'd dented his ego, aroused his curiosity, and seduced his imagination in just under fifteen minutes.

His pleasant expression faded when he saw Libby. Clad in a shapeless greatcoat that looked as though it should have been abandoned at Valley Forge, and wearing enormous glasses that hid half her face, she resembled a nearsighted mouse trapped in the folds of a heavy blanket.

"Are you lost, Mr. Stratton? I'd be happy to direct you to your hotel."

He ignored her question and her offer. "What's with the disguise?"

Libby stopped breathing, and her heart skittered to an abrupt halt.

"What are you hiding from, Libby Kincaid?"

Her nerves and her self-protective instincts went to full alert, but she simply gave him a wide-eyed I-don't-know-what-you-mean look. "Hiding?"

"Yes. Hiding. I'd be happy to spell the word and give you a definition, but I doubt it's necessary. Animal or vegetable, Libby Kincaid? Who or what are you hiding from in that getup?"

Even in the dim light of a nearby street lamp, Jake saw vibrant spots of color blossom on her cheeks. He knew a moment of regret that he'd embarrassed her, but she provoked the aggressive side of his nature without even trying. He ignored his conscience when it told him to back off. He also reasoned that if he had to get her mad in order to understand her, then so be it. He'd get her mad. Why he was willing to go to such lengths didn't even seem to matter any longer.

Associate Professor Libby Kincaid challenged him, and Jake Stratton thrived on challenges.

"I'm not hiding anything. My life's an open book. As the old saying goes, what you see is what you get."

"Try again."

She exhaled, the sound absurdly soft. Jake felt as though he had just kicked a helpless puppy. He also felt compelled to promise her that he'd protect her from the things she feared most. Stunned by the impulse, he remained silent.

"It's late, and I have to get home."

Jake seized her wrist as she walked past him. Normal small-town night sounds—a car door slamming, a distant ambulance siren wailing, a mother urging her recalcitrant child indoors for the night—provided background harmony to the tension humming between them.

Jake didn't ease his hold on her as she stared up at him. He felt his body respond to her even before he brought her flush against him. Baffled that a woman who seemed determined to look and behave like an old maid could mangle his common sense and rouse his senses so thoroughly, he refused to acknowledge the tension emanating from her or the shock in her eyes.

Libby took shallow breaths. She kept her expression neutral while she absorbed the impact of Jake Stratton's forceful personality. She saw anger and determination, and something else she couldn't even begin to identify, in his hard features.

She wanted to hate him. The heat and hardness of his body seduced her, though, and chased away her desire to summon even a single negative emotion.

"Mr. Stratton," she said quietly, unaware of the stark vulnerability on her face, "we're both tired and a little on edge right now, so why don't we simply say good night and get a fresh start in the morning?"

Anger renewed its claim on him. "You've got a body that doesn't quit, and you're hiding it under a thousand yards of fabric." To prove his point, Jake gripped her hips and brought her into contact with his pelvis. He ignored the tiny sound of surprise that escaped her. "You've got a couple of feet of what I suspect is hair like silk knotted up so tight that you're giving yourself a headache. You wear glasses that conceal most of your face, but they can't hide those blue ponds you've got for eyes. Why?" he demanded.

Patience gone, Libby jerked free of him, but she didn't run. Only cowards ran from a confrontation. And she wasn't a coward. She'd proven that to herself long ago.

Before she could speak her mind, Jake assaulted Libby from an unexpected angle. He felt the shock that held her immobile and the warmth of her skin when he ran his finger down her cheek. All the heat in their bodies seemed to coalesce at the point of contact.

When he finally paused at the pulse hammering in her throat and pressed his fingertips to the throbbing evidence of her hidden passion and obvious fury, he saw her eyes widen with surprise and heard what he hoped was a muted cry of desire. The scent of honeysuckle, a fragrance that seemed uniquely Libby, seduced him anew.

"You've got incredible skin," he told her in a low, seductive voice. "And your eyes are unbelievable. You've probably never cut your hair, so it's likely down to your hips. Why do you want to look like some damn wallflower? What are you hiding?"

Emotionally unstrung, Libby eased back from his touch. Jake reluctantly lowered his hand, but the tips of his fingers still burned from contact with her warm skin.

She inhaled deeply, holding air in her lungs until it burned and forced her to exhale. "I'm not hiding from anything or anyone," she insisted.

"Yes, you are, even if only from yourself. And unless you're the sole support of a dozen children, you don't have to go around looking like some reject from Goodwill. I'm not stupid, Libby Kincaid."

Jake knew he'd blundered when he saw the stunned look of her face. It was obvious to him that no one paid much attention to her or cared enough about her to question her behavior. Why any woman would conceal her natural assets puzzled him, and he wanted to understand her motivation.

"You may not be stupid, Mr. Stratton, but you are thoroughly tactless and remarkably rude."

Jake laughed. He mentally applauded her spirit. He savored the fire blazing in her huge eyes. And he loved the idea of stoking that fire until it produced an inferno capable of engulfing them both. He also wanted to comfort her, antagonize her, and tease her.

He covered his regret that he'd hurt her with his next comment. "I have a reputation for shooting from the hip. I guess you could say I don't like games."

She laughed back at him, the sound cynical and faintly derisive. "Sure you do. Look, I read the newspapers. Your life is one enormous Monopoly game interspersed with parties for the rich and famous. Ergo, you *love* games."

Jake hid his reaction to her comments. Intellectually, he understood her reasoning. Many people assumed that he was just another wheeler-dealer with an eye for the bottom line.

Those who knew him, however, knew the truth. He loathed the image the media had created for him, but he tried to live with it. Oddly, though, he felt a keen sense of disappointment that Libby Kincaid refused to let herself see beyond the distorted press reports. Without knowing it, she had targeted his secret vulnerability.

"Preconceived notions are often inaccurate, Libby."

She quelled her disbelief and her frustration with great effort. She also ignored the hurt that flashed briefly in his eyes before he schooled his expression to a look of aloof disinterest.

"Perhaps," she conceded, willing to accept that her preconceived notions could, in fact, be inaccurate. In his case, though, she needed to believe he was some irresponsible character who expected her to massage his ego. How else, she wondered, would she be able to dismiss the attraction she felt to him?

Suddenly very subdued, Jake asked, "You want me to request an alternate liaison person, don't you?"

Startled by his question, Libby nonetheless shook her head. She knew she couldn't afford to alienate Dean Cassidy or Avery Mendenhall over a personality dispute with a guest lecturer. "No, I don't. What I really want is an end to this verbal sniping."

He stuck out his hand, his expression calm and unthreatening. "Truce?"

She searched his face for some meaning behind the word, some hint that he might be toying with her. When she saw nothing suspicious, she accepted his gesture of conciliation. Once again, he scorched her skin with his touch. Alarmed, Libby quickly withdrew her hand, but his warmth stayed with her.

"Truce," she agreed breathlessly. "I'll see you in the morning then."

Libby turned and started down the sidewalk. Jake promptly joined her. He tucked his arm through hers, his long-legged stride forcing her to move at a brisk pace as they walked the two and a half blocks to her home.

Silent, resigned to his company, and unwilling

to challenge him again, Libby grappled with the confusing emotions he inspired.

A faint smile lifted the edges of her mouth when they were less than a block from her front door. She realized that she'd already devised a way to keep Jake Stratton from tampering with her schedule. She took comfort in the fact that the agenda she'd created for him would keep him very, very busy.

How else, she wondered, could she reasonably be expected to handle a man who effortlessly penetrated years of well-constructed reserve, kindled needs and thoughts within her that were too foolish to consider, and provoked her temper past the point of reason?

When they were on the front porch, Libby dug through her purse in search of her keys. Jake stood beside her, his presence making her clumsy. He didn't speak as she fumbled through the contents of her shoulder bag, but she felt the probing sweep of his gaze and sensed that he was studying her. She went weak with relief when she found her key ring.

A bright light flared as she slid the key into the lock. Startled, Libby glanced to her right. A figure emerged from the dark. Light flashed in her face a second and a third time, momentarily blinding her.

Blinking against the glare, she heard Jake mutter something coarse regarding the parentage of photographers before he snatched the key ring from her suddenly nerveless fingers. Another series of brilliant white flashes promptly reduced her vision to a cascade of exploding stars against a black canvas.

She didn't protest when Jake quickly jerked open the door, shoved her inside, and then slammed it shut. Arms extended to maintain her balance and blinking rapidly, she whirled about to peer through the glass section of the front door.

She saw Jake racing across her front lawn, in pursuit, she assumed, of the person who had burst out of nowhere and photographed them.

Her shock started to subside. She secured the lock on her front door and turned off the porch light with a growing smile of satisfaction. Libby silently blessed the unknown party wielding camera and flash attachment. After all her worrying for two and a half blocks about how to politely get rid of Jake Stratton, a member of the paparazzi that apparently trailed after him wherever he went had solved the problem for her.

Certain that she'd seen the last of him until their scheduled meeting the following morning, Libby decided that she could, and would, dismiss Jake Stratton from her mind. As she undressed and prepared for bed, she soon realized that eliminating him from her thoughts was far easier said than done.

Less than a block and a half from Libby Kincaid's front porch, Jake closed in on the photographer. He reached out and grabbed the fleeing man by the collar of his jacket. Jerking him around, Jake immediately seized his camera.

"Don't break it, Mr. Stratton. Please."

Jake glared down at him, his breathing surprisingly even given the speed at which he had pursued the younger man.

"I didn't mean any harm. Honest."

"You frightened the lady, and you invaded her privacy."

"I did my job."

"Which is?"

The photographer shifted nervously. "You're a celebrity, Mr. Stratton."

"What I'm not is a piece of meat hanging in a butcher's shop window."

Mortified, the young man agreed, "No, sir, you're not."

"Who do you work for?"

"I mostly free-lance."

Jake began to fiddle with the back of the camera, his intent obvious.

"Mr. Stratton, please."

"Talk," Jake ordered, his expression grim.

"*Celebrity Beat,* but I'm just a temporary stringer. The reporter who hired me said shooting you would get me an interview for a job."

Jake knew the sleazy tabloid. He breathed an unrepeatable oath before asking, "How old are you?"

"Nineteen."

"Still in school?"

"Only part time."

"Why?"

"I have to earn my tuition and room and board."

Jake resented the young man's tone, which implied that he didn't understand sacrifice or struggle, but he opted not to set him straight. "I'll make you a deal."

"How do I know I can trust you?"

"You don't," Jake assured him bluntly.

The young man considered what he knew about Jake Stratton and made a quick decision. "What's the deal?"

"Destroy this film right now, and respect Professor Kincaid's privacy." He noted the horrified look on the photographer's face. "In exchange, I'll guarantee a private session with candid photographs and an interview if you'll forget your aspirations of working for *Celebrity Beat*. You'll do yourself far more good professionally by marketing your exclusive with me to a more reputable magazine."

"But that puts you in control of everything!" the photographer exclaimed.

Jake hefted the camera positioned precariously in his right hand, a reminder that he *was* in control of the situation. "It also allows you a chance to exercise your conscience."

The young man appeared reluctant, but Jake saw no reason to attempt additional persuasion.

"You've got yourself a deal, Mr. Stratton, but I reserve the right to cover anything newsworthy that may come up while you're here."

Jake nodded, flipped open the compartment at the back of the camera, and exposed the undeveloped film. He almost smiled when he heard the young photographer groan. Jake could appreciate the boy's momentary despair, but he had no desire to spend the next six weeks dodging every clump of shrubbery in Hancock, Illinois.

He returned the camera, learned the young

man's name, and gave him a business card with his private number in Chicago before retracing his steps to Libby's small house. He doubted that she'd retired for the night, despite the fact that all the lights in the front portion of her home were off.

Jake made his way around to the rear of the house. He paused at the kitchen door and peered through the glass panel into what he knew most people called the heart of a home. He felt somewhat unsettled by the sudden realization that his penthouse in Chicago lacked an essential warmth that so many people simply took for granted.

Unwilling to wallow in such melancholy thoughts, Jake focused on Libby. Seated at a small table for two, a mug wedged between her hands, she wore a shabby bathrobe unsuited to a woman whose body could seduce during the briefest contact.

He nonetheless smiled at her attire, but his smile slowly faded when he noticed the hauntingly wistful expression on her face. With her long hair unbound and her glasses no longer obscuring her facial features, she looked stunningly innocent, profoundly vulnerable, and so lovely, his insides ached. Protective instincts surfaced inside him, and a current of desire that startled him.

He resisted the stark realization that the look on her face reminded him of the loneliness he often experienced. Still, he couldn't deny the reality that, while his professional endeavors were lauded around the globe, he had no one with whom to share his triumphs or to mourn the few failures that had cut deeply into his soul.

Libby shifted in her chair, an action that sent

her dense mane of dark hair sliding silkily across one shoulder.

Jake again felt raw desire surge to life in every molecule of his body as he watched her. Marrow-deep hunger sliced right through every self-protective barrier he possessed like a newly sharpened knife. He felt like a schoolboy with tattered nerves. She teased the control he insisted on in all facets of his life, making him unexpectedly angry that an innocent like Libby Kincaid could arouse and torment him with such provocative ease.

For a moment he deeply resented her. In the next moment he craved her naked body and the passion he sensed she would bring to a lover.

Three

Jake pounded on the door, his aggressive emotions producing a forcefulness that threatened to shatter the glass panel. He drew great satisfaction from the fact that he startled Libby, but a moment later he felt childish and petulant for crediting her with seduction when all she really seemed to want to do was avoid him.

Get yourself together, he warned himself, or you'll scare her right into a convent.

Libby's shock was genuine. Caught up in a foolish and embarrassingly erotic fantasy that involved Jake, she felt guilty, as though she were a four-year-old caught stealing penny candy.

Eyes riveted on Jake, she abandoned her chair, nearly upending it as she jumped to her feet and headed for the back door. She paused halfway across the room, the wisdom of letting him into her home so late at night giving her pause.

Reluctantly easing open the door, she studied

him with the same wary fascination that most people devote to snakes and guns. "Are you lost?" she asked hopefully.

He laughed, the crow's-feet around his gray eyes forming an appealing pattern as his grin widened with genuine delight. "Don't ever change, Libby. You're one of a kind."

Flustered, she stiffened. She also made no move to step out of the way and invite him inside. Closing her graceful hands into tight fists in an effort to keep from reaching out and trailing her fingertips along the alluring line of his mustache, she fumbled for something appropriate to say. "It's late, and I'm about to retire for the night."

Jake leaned negligently against the doorframe and regarded her with that mocking half-smile of his that made all her nerve endings stand on end. Libby glared at him. She refused to budge while she endured his inspection, although she could have bitten her tongue for using a word like "retire." She knew it made her sound like some prissy old maid in a Victorian novel. Her conscience told her that that was precisely what she was becoming.

"Are we going to have a stare-down, Libby?"

"Not if you leave," she shot back.

His smile dimmed. "I don't want to leave. Not yet, anyway. Aren't you curious about the guy who jumped out of your hedge?"

She shook her head, although she was secretly fascinated by what had happened. She was also curious to know how Jake hand handled the situation.

"I caught up with him. We had a very interesting chat. I doubt he'll bother you again."

As he spoke, Jake eased inside the kitchen, moving toward Libby cautiously. Unaware of what she was actually doing, she stepped back a pace.

"He didn't bother me," she insisted.

Jake eyed her curiously. "He didn't?"

"Of course not. He was taking your picture, not mine." In spite of her determination not to admit her curiosity, she heard herself ask, "Does that kind of thing happen to you very often?"

He shrugged and inched nearer. "Often enough."

She noticed the distaste in his expression as she drifted to one side of the door. Compassion flirted with her instinctive resistance to him, though she struggled not to feel any positive or sympathetic emotions for him.

"You're not used to it by now?"

"I like my privacy."

"Most people do," she commented, compassion toppling the first stone from her wall of resistance. Her heart thudded crazily as she watched him. Taking an unsteady breath, and then another, she didn't realize that Jake watched with fascination the erratic rise and fall of her breasts. "But I guess it comes with the territory. After all, you're what they call a media superstar, aren't you?"

She saw him flinch and was surprised by his reaction.

"I'm a businessman, Libby. Nothing more, nothing less."

"But people think you're much more than that."

"Not with my encouragement."

"Oh."

Libby absently watched Jake take hold of the door and slide it closed. Finally realizing that he'd finessed his way right into her home, she shivered and wrapped her arms around her waist. "You're also very sneaky, aren't you?"

He grinned, and Libby glimpsed the mischievous boy he'd once been. Several additional stones tumbled from her inner wall.

"I'm just a sucker for hot cocoa."

"Are you sure you don't mean cognac?"

He shook his head. "There you go again, Professor," he chided. "You're drawing conclusions about me that have no basis in fact."

Libby thought he looked somewhat melancholy. "One cup of cocoa," she warned as she went to the refrigerator for milk. "But then you'll have to be on your way."

"Yes, ma'am."

She hesitated at the refrigerator door, hating that she sounded like a drill instructor barking orders at him, and hating, too, that she would have to send him away. Glancing back over her shoulder, she watched him settle into a chair at the table. With his long legs and large frame, he dwarfed the furniture.

Libby stared at him for a long moment, trying to come to terms with the fact that he was here in her kitchen and she was in her tackiest bathrobe. She nervously tucked the scarlet lace edge of her nightgown down past the collar of her robe as she reached for the milk. She considered her very feminine lingerie her one private luxury in an otherwise simple life, and she wondered if that kind of indulgence made her appear foolish to a sophisticated man like Jake Stratton.

"If you'd prefer, I think I have some sherry," she commented in an effort to seem composed.

"Cocoa's fine. It's getting colder out at night. We'll probably have our first snowfall fairly soon."

Libby paced the width of the stove while the milk heated. She felt like a fool, but she couldn't seem to stop moving back and forth while she tried to figure out how to cope with Jake's presence, his probing gaze, and her insane reaction to him.

"You're starting to remind me of a sentry on guard duty. Relax," he suggested quietly. "I don't bite, and I'm not looking for a hostage."

She pressed her back against the edge of the stove, her eyes as big as saucers and her hands clenched together so he wouldn't notice their slight trembling.

"If you'll tell me what I'm doing that's making you so nervous, I'll be able to stop it."

Libby heard his sincerity. A gust of air escaped her before she admitted, "You're not doing anything. I'm just a little edgy, that's all, and I don't know what to say to you." She registered his surprise as she turned to check the milk, which had finally started to bubble.

Libby used a whisk to blend in the powdered cocoa while she frantically plumbed her brain for something clever to say. Taking the saucepan from the stove, she held the mug steady with her free hand and began to pour the steaming cocoa.

"You've got incredible hair."

She jumped at the sound of his low voice, sloshed hot cocoa across her fingers, and let out a muffled cry. Libby heard a chair scrape across the tile floor. She didn't protest when Jake relieved her of the pan, guided her to the sink, and carefully bathed her fingers in cold tap water.

Head bowed, Libby closed her eyes and tried to fight back the tears stinging her eyes—tears of embarrassment, not pain.

"Is the water helping?" he asked.

She nodded, aware that she'd be a fool to even attempt speech. Thirty years old, she silently berated herself, and you can't even hold a conversation with a man without scalding yourself. Caught up in her own self-disgust, Libby didn't know she was shaking so badly that Jake was afraid to release her.

He turned off the water, helped himself to a clean towel from a stack on the counter, and gently guided Libby toward the table. He sat down, trapping her between his sturdy thighs. Watching him, Libby felt a certain awe at the tender way in which he dried her fingers and then inspected them for burns.

She sensed the leashed power of his body, and she felt the muscles that held her captive. She shivered delicately, and then she whispered, "I'm all right. It doesn't hurt."

He glanced at her, his expression startlingly sober and strained. "You're afraid of me."

Libby didn't miss the shock underscoring his observation. "No!"

"You don't like me."

"No! Yes!"

"Which is it?"

"I don't know!" she exclaimed, although she

really did know. Honesty finally compelled her to admit, "I don't want to like you, but I think I do."

"And that's so awful?" Jake pressed, clearly bewildered. "You don't want to want me, either, but you do."

She frowned as she studied him. And she wondered why he couldn't be the superficial egomaniac she wanted him to be. The fact that he had her wedged between his muscular thighs kept escalating her discomfort. She knew she should put as much distance between them as possible, but she couldn't seem to move. Nor did she really want to.

In her heart of hearts Libby craved the caring and concern shining in Jake's eyes, but she reminded herself that he probably felt nothing but pity for her clumsy display and inelegant appearance. Without her knowing it, her frown deepened.

"Didn't your mother ever tell you that frowning will give you premature wrinkles?" he teased playfully.

Libby went perfectly still for a long moment. She felt her heart start to gallop in her chest. Heat rushed to the surface of her skin. Confusion raged inside her, but it didn't keep her from speaking words she'd never uttered to another living soul.

"My mother was never sober long enough to offer advice while I was growing up." Shocked by her own candor, she tried to turn away, but Jake wouldn't allow her to escape. She felt his hands tighten on her waist. "I don't believe I just said that," she managed in a strangled voice.

"I've heard worse, Libby. And I've seen worse."

She raised her chin, arranged her posture like a

soldier's at attention, and dared him with her eyes to make one sympathetic sound. "I don't want your pity. I do, however, want you to leave."

Jake ignored her second comment. "I have a lot of mixed feelings where you're concerned, but pity definitely isn't one of them."

"I expect you to keep it that way."

He grinned at her prim order.

"Don't do that! Those blasted smiles of yours are absolutely blinding. You're going to give me a migraine." She scowled at him, although she had trouble sustaining the cloudy expression for very long.

He laughed out loud and brought her against his powerful body in a bear hug. His laughter soon turned to a groan as she squirmed against his groin. When he could speak, he said, "I like you, Libby Kincaid, but I'm starting to think you're part tiger and part sorceress."

"I'm neither." Her tone was crisp enough to cause a severe case of frostbite. "What I am is an associate professor of business communications, and your liaison person for exactly six weeks."

He shrugged, the gesture deceptively careless. "You're a woman, and I'm a man."

Like I need to be reminded that you're a man, Libby nearly groaned aloud.

As if to prove his point, Jake slid his fingers through the cascade of dark hair that reached her waist. Libby trembled. The warmth of his body enveloped her, while the scent of his after-shave tantalized her imagination. She knew she had to call a halt to this insanity, but Jake spoke before she could chastise him for his familiar manner.

"I was right, you know. Touching your hair is like plunging my hands into yards and yards of the finest silk."

His words made her knees weak, but she gave him a stern look. "Do you sweet-talk *every* woman you meet?"

Drowning in a flash flood of exquisite sensations as he repeatedly slid his fingers through the density of her long hair, Jake neither heard nor responded to Libby's question.

Libby, on the other hand, felt her bones start to soften. The blood moving through her veins became sluggish. Emotions she didn't even know she possessed burst across the landscape of her consciousness with all the subtlety of exploding dynamite and paralyzed her ability to reason. Suddenly panicked, she pulled free of Jake. She retreated to the stove and started making hot cocoa all over again.

Jake fought his body for control and pondered her in silence. He suspected that he should leave her in peace, but he liked being in her homey kitchen. He also liked the incinerating heat charging through his veins. He felt more alive than he'd felt in years.

He silently studied the lace peeking from the collar of her worn robe. It intrigued him, because if seemed at odds with the persona she revealed to the world. He forced himself to ignore the throbbing urge that encouraged him to bury his face in the luxurious curtain of silk hair, but he couldn't banish the tension that threatened to overwhelm him.

More certain than ever that Libby was hiding

from something or someone, Jake promised himself that he would accept the challenge inherent in her determined aloofness. He shifted in his chair, still physically uncomfortable from the arousal he felt for a woman he barely knew.

The incongruity of the situation wasn't lost on him. He couldn't recall the last time he'd pursued a woman. Women generally pursued him, but they grasped the ground rules from the start. Most knew about his divorce several years earlier, and most understood his unwillingness to complicate his life with anything more than the companionship of worldly, career-committed women who accepted the boundaries he placed on relationships.

Libby Kincaid might be innocent and awkward, but she also possessed the seductive appeal of Eve. A part of him wanted an immediate and intimate sample of the woman hidden behind ugly clothing and a combative nature.

The part of him that should have questioned the wisdom of pursuing a sensitive and inexperienced woman remained silent in the face of a perceived challenge. His common sense finally asserted itself, however, and he forced himself to relax as Libby brought two mugs filled with fresh cocoa to the table.

Seated opposite Jake at the small table, Libby reminded herself one final time that he was unpredictable, far too self-assured, overwhelmingly sexy, and thoroughly dangerous to a woman who knew nothing of the games played by worldly men and women. She also renewed her vow not to allow him to jeopardize the successful completion of her textbook or the smooth flow of her teaching schedule.

"What kind of schedule do we have ahead of us?"

Libby almost gave him a gold star for picking the one subject she was willing to discuss. "An extremely well rounded one. Of course, you'll utilize the basic schedule Dean Cassidy approved for you. I've also planned time at the library and local bookstores so that you can sign copies of your book." She smiled at him before continuing.

"Numerous students from the Entrepreneurship in Business class have signed up for informal weekly group sessions with you. There are several fraternity- and sorority-sponsored teas, in addition to an alumni luncheon being held in your honor. You'll probably want to write a speech for the luncheon since you'll be receiving an award. The campus TV station wants to interview you, as well as the local media, of course. And then there's the . . ." She paused when Jake finished his cocoa in one long gulp and got to his feet.

"Time for me to get some sleep. It sounds like I'm going to be busy."

Although surprised by his abruptness, Libby beamed. "I was sure you wouldn't want too many free hours. I know you're accustomed to a full schedule."

He smiled back at her, but his smile was slightly off center because he was also grinding his teeth together.

Libby followed him to the door. "Is there anything else you'd like me to add to your schedule?"

Jake shook his head. "Definitely not. I have every confidence that you've done exactly what you thought best under the circumstances. Just make sure I get a copy of my itinerary."

"Certainly."

"It really sounds just great," he continued with false sincerity, "and very thorough. In fact, I'm amazed by just how thorough you've been."

Casting a questioning look in his direction, she pulled open the kitchen door and asked, "Is something wrong, Jake?"

His gaze narrowed, his expression growing stormier by the second. Libby stuffed her hands into the pockets of her robe and shifted uncomfortably under the force of his penetrating look.

"Libby?" he said so softly that she had to strain to hear him.

She looked up at him, all innocence and bright-eyed curiosity. "Yes?"

Jake leaned down. Libby held very still. She stared at his mouth and wondered again what his mustache felt like.

"Never try to outfox a fox," he whispered just before he lowered his mouth to hers and tasted what he'd wanted to taste since their first few moments together.

She instinctively stiffened with shock and disbelief, but chemistry and desire and Jake Stratton fully devastated her resistance.

She held her breath as he tenderly explored the shape and texture of her lips. When she finally released the air trapped in her lungs, he greedily inhaled it into his own mouth. Libby moaned, but there was no protest in the erotic sound. Heat pooled inside her and then spread in ever-widening circles to consume her.

She suddenly felt reckless and out of control. She felt profoundly shocked by what was happening. She felt eager and hungry and wanton. She also felt dangerously faint.

Jake kept her upright when her knees started to buckle. Libby experienced an almost feverish desire to touch him, but his embrace prevented her from freeing hands still jammed into the pockets of her robe.

As though aware of her desire, Jake cradled her face in his palms, slanted his mouth across hers, and mounted a sensual assault. Libby eagerly welcomed the thrust of his tongue as it slipped past her parted lips and into the secret flavors and textures of her mouth.

She moaned again. She also feared being labeled a fool for her receptivity to his unexpected passion, but she couldn't find the strength to end this moment of madness.

He taunted her. He aroused her. And then he released her just as suddenly as he had seized her.

They stared at each other, both breathless and flushed, both simmering with desire, and both stunned by what they'd just shared.

Libby couldn't speak. She simply stared at Jake, her eyes huge with shock and her lips swollen and damp from his kisses as her body trembled violently.

He opened his mouth to speak. His lips moved, but the words refused to emerge. He cleared his throat, threw his head back, and inhaled sharply against the agonized condition of his body. It took a few minutes, but he finally reclaimed his grasp on reality.

Gently tapping Libby on the end of her nose, he spoke in a husky tone of voice that defeated his attempt at playfulness. "Lock your door. There are all kinds of crazies on the streets at night." *And I'm one of them*, he finished silently.

The sound of the door being slammed shut jolted Libby from her dazed state. Armed only with her fragmented emotions, she automatically made her way to the table, collected the mugs they'd used, rinsed them and left them in the sink, and then went to bed.

Her shock slowly waned. In its wake were regret and embarrassment and unsatisfied hunger, as well as the realization that Jake Stratton had touched more than her heart. He had begun to breach the barrier that protected her soul.

Four

Too restless to sleep, Libby abandoned her bed shortly before dawn. She showered and dressed, made a pot of strong tea, and then tried to devote the quiet of the early morning hours to editing the most recently written chapter of her textbook.

Thoughts of Jake intruded on her concentration, despite her best efforts to dismiss him from her mind. A realist, Libby refused to lie to herself. She knew that the disparity in their lifestyles and backgrounds made her completely unsuitable for a dynamic and worldly man like Jake Stratton, even if he did fascinate her.

She also knew she couldn't let it matter that he roused long-dormant needs and dreams deep within her, fired her blood to fever pitch, and sent her imagination about his potential as a lover into overdrive. Risking the emotional equilibrium she'd finally achieved would be disastrous.

What had happened between them the previous

night was, she decided, a fluke. One of those crazy situations that occur when defenses crumble and common sense flies out the window. To justify her conclusions, Libby decided that Jake probably felt as awkward about the situation as she did.

As she left her house for the short drive to his hotel, she promised herself that she would behave as though nothing out of the ordinary had taken place between them. With the confidence inspired by her renewed determination, she decided she could maintain the control needed to handle Jake Stratton.

The fear and loneliness she'd endured as a child had taught her the necessity of setting the tone of all her adult relationships. Those she couldn't orchestrate she simply abandoned. Dealing with Jake wouldn't be quite so simple, of course, but the survivor within her refused to give up. One way or another, she would win the battle.

She spotted him the instant she walked into the hotel lobby. He stood at the concierge's desk, his expression a study in concentration as he spoke into the phone. Squaring her shoulders and gripping the handle of her leather satchel so tightly that her knuckles turned white, Libby approached him with the attitude and posture of a soldier going into battle.

She couldn't help wondering about Carol, the woman to whom he spoke with such warmth and compassion. She wondered if a man would ever speak to her in just that way, and then she rejected the notion. Only in her dreams, she realized. Only in her dreams.

The sound of Jake's voice began to gnaw on her

resistance to him. Her resolve to maintain her emotional distance started to unravel. He'd used that seductive tone of voice on her the previous night. It had routed her common sense and turned her bones to soft putty.

A burst of fury detonated within her. Libby inhaled sharply in an effort to steady herself as she studied him, but he still took her breath away. Her body felt all flushed and hungry, and she could feel her skin singing with awareness.

Without wanting to, she recalled with total clarity the encompassing safety of his embrace, the gentleness of his hands as he'd cradled her face in them, the musk-scented warmth of his skin, and the sensuality of his mouth when he'd kissed her. And the seductive, compelling taste of him. She shuddered, realizing just how much she loved the very taste of him.

She also remembered that his mustache was softer than she'd expected. Almost like the whisper of butterfly wings against her skin. Her last thought made her insides clench.

Jake selected that moment to replace the receiver and smile at Libby. "Good morning, Little Professor."

His teasing brought her crashing back to earth. Libby suddenly wanted to throttle him for it, but she smiled pleasantly instead. "Shall we get to work? We have a busy day and a lot of territory to cover."

Jake took note of the dreary wool jumper she wore and the tortured state of her beautiful hair. "Sure, but not here. I've got just the spot for us, and we won't be disturbed."

He relieved her of her briefcase, took her arm, and hustled her out of the hotel at top speed. Libby barely had time to protest. She finally jerked free of him when they reached her car. Jake frowned. Libby didn't want to acknowledge the problem, but it was too obvious to ignore.

"We'll take my car," he announced.

She reluctantly nodded, but only because she couldn't fault his reasoning. He'd have to twist himself into a pretzel just to fit into the front seat of her tiny imported vehicle. She remained quiet and ignored his curious glances as he summoned a young man from valet parking.

Settled in Jake's car a few minutes later, Libby said, "Avery Mendenhall isn't expecting us until midmorning, so we'll have a chance to go over your agenda in detail before we meet with him."

"Wonderful. There are a few points I think we should discuss." He pulled out of the hotel's driveway and into light morning traffic.

Libby exhaled softly, pleased by his low-key attitude. Glancing at him, she reacquainted herself with his strong jaw and rugged profile. Her nerve endings fluttered wildly. She nearly groaned, but she managed to bite her tongue in time and get herself under control. Suppressing the urge to thank Jake for not saying a word about the previous night, she quickly decided that the situation was best forgotten.

She watched him flip a lever on the dashboard. A moment later the opening strains of the 1812 Overture filled the air. Although surprised that they shared the same taste in music, she started to relax for the first time that morning.

Lost in the beauty of Tchaikovsky's music, Libby belatedly noticed two things. Jake knew his way around Hancock, which really didn't surprise her, since he'd lived in the small college town several years earlier and it hadn't changed much with the passage of time. The second thing she noticed, the part that alarmed her, was that he was driving away from the campus, not toward it.

"Where are we going?" she enunciated carefully.

"Trust me."

"You haven't earned my trust," she said bluntly, panic rising up inside her like an acid tide.

Jake glanced in her direction when he paused at a Stop sign. "Still mad about last night? Look, just relax and enjoy the ride. I promise you won't be disappointed."

"Kidnapping is against the law, Mr. Stratton." She paused, tried to relax, and then said in a tight little voice, "I don't wish to discuss last night. As far as I'm concerned, it didn't happen."

He chuckled, but there was little humor in the sound. "I beg to differ, Libby, my love."

She flinched, but not because she didn't want to be someone's "love." She simply couldn't handle being used as the butt of anyone's humor when her emotions were involved. "Don't call me that."

"Why not?"

She didn't notice the sudden flash of concern in Jake's eyes. Something very fragile deep inside her unexpectedly snapped, prompting her to express feelings she'd buried for years.

"I'm nobody's love. Do you think I'm blind? Well, I'm not. I know what stares back at me when I look in a mirror. You don't have to flatter me, or feed my ego, or make me think I'm something special. It's not required or necessary. I'll get you through this lecture series free of charge, so you can just cease and desist immediately with all your game-playing and meaningless attention."

Pain surged into her skull. Frustrated, Libby slammed her hand against the dashboard. The 1812 Overture died with a squeak. "Now I'm getting a headache."

Jake reached over and plucked two enormous hairpins from her hair, the expression on his face grim. "Then quit torturing yourself."

Her hair tumbled everywhere, into her face, across her shoulders, and down her arms. Ashamed of her loss of control and so angry with Jake that she couldn't think clearly, she watched him pull off the main road. She made no attempt to restrain her hair. Her shock mounted when he continued down a rutted gravel road, instead of turning the car around and heading back to town.

"You're a sadist," she burst out. Tears glittered on her eyelashes like fine crystal shards, but she refused to cry in front of him. "A total sadist. I should have known better than to get into a car with you."

One of his dark brows rose. "Sadist's the wrong word, Libby. Find another."

Libby fumed silently. Provoked, Jake grabbed her chin with his right hand and forced her to look at him. "Try friend, coworker, or maybe even lover, but quit acting like I'm the enemy. We both know I'm not."

Furious, she wrenched free and sidled up to the

passenger door. "You are the most arrogant, despicable—"

"You've got quite a temper," he noted mildly. "But then I figured that out last night."

She shot him a look that would have crippled any other man. "You obviously bring out the best in people."

Jake said nothing more, but a muscle ticked violently in his jaw as he eased the car off the gravel road and brought it to a stop in a small glade. Turning, he seized Libby by the arms and held her still while she glared at him.

He hated the smudges of fatigue under her eyes, and he drew little satisfaction from the fact that neither one of them had slept much the previous night. But, even more, he loathed the fear she failed to conceal behind the fire in her anger-filled eyes.

"Remove your hands from my body."

He ignored her order even as he felt the tremors shaking her, and he fought the urge to draw her against his body and provide her with a safe harbor. He knew this wasn't the time, but he promised himself he would find the right time.

"You're right, Libby. I *do* bring out the best in you, because I arouse your passion. But that scares the living daylights out of you, doesn't it?"

All the muscles in her slender body suddenly went slack. He tightened his hold on her and kept her upright in the passenger seat, but he saw that he'd scored a bull's-eye.

Libby groaned, anger, shock, and humiliation coursing through her as her eyelids fluttered closed.

Jake breathed something distinctly profane.

Her eyes snapped open and her chin trembled, but she managed to speak. "Don't you dare swear at me."

He released her. "Dammit, I'm not swearing at you."

"Of course you are!" she exclaimed. "You just did."

Jake shoved open his door and got out of the car. He counted to ten as he walked around to Libby's side of the vehicle, opened the passenger door, and tugged her to her feet.

"Don't move." He released her long enough to shut the car door. With a gentleness that surprised them both, he lifted his hands and arranged her hair so that it tumbled down her back.

His fingertips lingered on the vulnerable curve of her neck, and he watched a slow flush of color blossom just beneath the surface of her skin. In that moment he wondered if her nipples were the same delicate shade of pink. Jake inhaled raggedly as he trailed his fingertips across her shoulders and down her arms. Although he longed to fill his hands with her breasts, he managed to keep them from straying when he saw the anxious expression on her face.

"Trust me, Libby. All I want is your trust."

She studied the twigs and leaves cluttering the ground, shaken by what she'd seen in Jake's eyes. "I don't trust people."

"But you want to, don't you?" he asked in a low voice.

She lifted her head. Jake saw the tears welling in her eyes, but he resisted the urge to comfort her.

"Take me back to town."

"I can't. We're here for breakfast."

Startled, she looked at him with an expression that clearly questioned his sanity. "In the woods?"

He took her hand. She didn't try to withdraw it, but the wariness of her posture prompted him to say, "I didn't bring you here to hurt you, to yell at you, or to seduce you."

"You're being manipulative," she accused quietly.

"No, I'm not. What I'm doing is making you a promise."

"You're still being manipulative." Her headache started to ease, and she awkwardly admitted, "I didn't have time for breakfast this morning."

What she wouldn't admit was that she'd been mooning over him since his departure the night before. Her common sense might not be too happy to see him, she realized, but her heart was pitifully overjoyed.

Jake took her last comment as a positive sign. "Stay put. I'll be right back."

She watched him open the trunk. "The food's in there?"

He produced a shawl of heather-shaded cashmere, which he draped across her shoulders. He lingered behind her, his hands buried in her long hair until Libby turned and gave him a curious look.

"It still feels like silk, and it smells faintly of honeysuckle blossoms in the spring."

She felt excruciatingly awkward and shy. "I sometimes rinse it with rainwater after I wash it."

"I can think of a half-dozen women who'd sell their souls for a mane like yours."

She shrugged. "Sounds pretty foolish to me."

Jake laughed at her innocence, but he wasn't making fun of her. He was simply amazed. Taking her by the hand, he guided her down a narrow trail through a section of dense foliage. "We need to renew our truce."

"I know." She glanced at him for a moment, genuinely startled by how kind and thoughtful he could be. She fingered the lush cashmere shawl with her free hand. She couldn't recall anyone ever being so concerned about her well-being. Nor could she recall ever having received a gift from a man.

"Consider our truce officially renewed," he ordered.

She smiled against her will. She liked him, she realized with surprise. Aside from the fact that she craved his touch and another sampling of his sensual nature, she *really* liked him. Even if he did act like Attila the Hun at times.

To cover her conflicted emotions, she remarked, "You are the bossiest man I've ever met."

"And you," he said quietly, "might think you've convinced the world that you're a mouse, but I know better. Your roar is something else, woman."

She favored him with a look she used on uncooperative students. It normally cowed them into instant submission. "I learned to stick up for myself a long time ago. It's not a lesson I intend to unlearn."

Jake exhaled heavily, an oddly sad sound that took her by surprise. "I think we both learned that particular lesson early on in life. We just use it differently, Libby. I want to know why."

She slowed her steps until Jake was forced to come to a stop beside her. "The past is over, so there's no need to dwell on it." *You wouldn't want to know me if you knew about my past.*

"I don't agree."

"Why doesn't that surprise me?" she asked rhetorically. "My life isn't a scavenger hunt, Jake, and my privacy is very important to me." His thoughtful expression gave her the courage to go on. "I overreacted earlier when I accused you of kidnapping me. It was a silly thing to say, and I apologize."

He squeezed her hand. "I think we both went a little crazy, but I did learn something important about you."

"What's that?" She averted her gaze and studied their entwined fingers. This means nothing, she told herself. Nothing. Her heart didn't want to believe her.

"There's someone very special hiding under all this armor you're hauling around. I'm going to find her, and then we're both going to enjoy her."

She stiffened. "You're not going to change me, so if you feel the need to rehabilitate something, find a crumbling building to work on."

He shook his head, his legendary stubbornness evident in his stance and his determined expression as he clamped his hands over her narrow shoulders. She stiffened. He waited patiently for her to relax. When she did, he told her, "You're a challenge, Libby, and I don't walk away from a challenge."

She eased out from under his grip and threw up her hands in complete frustration. "You're absolutely impossible."

He grabbed one of her hands and grinned down at her. "That's part of the Stratton charm."

She started to laugh. She couldn't help herself when she saw the twinkle in his warm gray eyes.

"You make me want to hug you, woman."

Her smiled faltered. "Let's not tempt fate. We can be friends, if you'd like, and we can work together, but that's it."

Jake listened carefully to what she didn't say. He heard a subtle undertone of fear behind her words. Frightening Libby wasn't a part of his agenda. Understanding her was. He promised himself that he would proceed with as much caution as he could muster with her.

Looking at her, he realized, was a lot like staring at a reflection of the emotional isolation he frequently experienced. She aroused his hunger for something more than the fast-track life he lived.

Dismissing his unsettling thoughts, he tugged her forward into a lovely, sun-dappled glade that hugged the edge of Hancock Lake. He smiled, awash in satisfaction when he heard her soft gasp of surprise.

"You approve?" Jake asked as he led her to a festive tent that housed a wicker table for two.

Wide-eyed with amazement, Libby noted the crisp white linen tablecloth, a mixed arrangement of wildflowers and blush roses in a vase atop the table, and place settings of the finest crystal and china. Even the white wicker chairs had plump seat cushions for comfort. A waiter stood near the table, a cart filled with covered dishes, and a silver bucket of iced champagne beside him.

"This is for us?" she clarified.

"Breakfast, as promised, Professor Kincaid."

"It's lovely, and very thoughtful, but why?"

Jake helped her into her chair and then seated himself opposite her before he answered. Candor, he decided, would be his best bet with her.

"I get the impression that no one's ever taught you how to relax. This is your first lesson." He nodded at the waiter, who moved forward to pour the champagne.

Libby nudged her pride aside and tried to forget how awkward and dowdy she appeared to someone like Jake. With quiet dignity, she said, "Thank you."

Jake smiled at her. "You deserve good things."

Amazed that he would think something like that, she nervously fingered the petals of the single long-stemmed blush rose positioned across the top of her plate as the waiter filled their goblets.

Champagne was something she considered reserved for lovers, weddings, and anniversaries. Having it with breakfast felt incredibly decadent. She wondered if verbalizing that feeling would serve to emphasize her lack of experience to Jake, so she kept her reaction to herself.

Completely at ease with the impromptu luxury of the setting he'd masterminded, Jake lifted his goblet in a toast. "To a successful lecture series."

She echoed his sentiment before taking a sip of the champagne. Tiny bubbles tickled her nose, and she smiled at the sensation.

"Friends and lovers. May we be both," he toasted a second time when their waiter turned away.

"Friends," Libby repeated, pretending he'd said nothing else.

Jake didn't try to manufacture conversation during the meal. Content to share the serenity of their surroundings, he sensed that Libby needed time to overcome her nervousness. He wanted her to feel indulged. It suddenly occurred to him that giving another person pleasure had not been a part of his personal goals in a very long time.

Jake experienced a moment of genuine puzzlement as he confronted his need to please Libby. He realized that her indifference to his celebrity status secretly charmed him, but her apparent determination to keep him from penetrating the facade she projected to the world, as well as her obvious desire to control their time together, also frustrated him.

He took limited consolation in the fact that he had jostled her world enough to catch a few glimpses of the real Libby Kincaid—the feisty creature willing to do battle with him when she felt threatened.

Her fire and her passion intrigued and aroused him. Instead of deflecting his attention, her temper, which was so at odds with her spinsterish demeanor, made him want to push her right over the edge just so he could see what would happen next. Her reserve kept triggering the switch marked "challenge" deep in the core of his being. Jake doubted that she was aware of the way her secrets beckoned him closer, even when she instinctively shied away from him.

Even time seemed inconsequential as a measurement of his relationship with Libby. He felt as though he'd always known her, always been hungry for her.

Studying her, he watched her smile at their waiter as the man poured her a second cup of coffee. Jake instantly coveted the spontaneity of her expression. He wondered why she refused to reveal herself to him without restraint, without the instinctive wariness that seemed an integral part of her nature.

Something tightened deep inside him, and he shifted uncomfortably in his chair. For a moment he resented the urgent hunger he felt for Libby. An unexpected sound, discordant when contrasted against the serenity of the glade, suddenly jarred him from his thoughts.

Startled, Libby almost choked on the plump strawberry she'd just popped into her mouth. She glanced at Jake as she groped for her water glass. His gaze narrowed speculatively when the foliage a few dozen yards away began to rustle. Branches snapped.

Jake got to his feet, dropped his linen napkin on the table, and forced himself to smile. "I doubt it's anything more annoying than a foraging animal." He suspected otherwise, but he didn't want to alarm Libby. "I'll be right back."

She nodded as she placed her water glass back on the table. "Be careful" slipped out before she could stop the words.

He grinned at her, blinding her yet again with a display of even white teeth. Feeling foolish, Libby studied the design engraved on her coffee cup with exaggerated interest as he rounded the table and came to a stop beside her chair.

Leaning down, Jake slid his hand under the weight of her thick hair. His blunt-tipped fingers came to rest at her nape, marking her with the scorching heat of his touch.

Flustered, Libby held very still. She watched him closely through a veil of thick, dark eyelashes, her heart racing. She finally whispered, "Is something wrong?"

"Nothing a kiss wouldn't cure."

She gave him a quick peck on the cheek.

"Wrong spot," he observed, forgetting briefly the noise at the edge of the glade that had drawn his attention.

Courage crept into her heart, stealthy and determined as it inspired her to discard her fear. She tentatively leaned forward and found his lips. And in doing so, she discovered that she had just willingly hurled herself into a whirlpool of sensation.

Jake struggled to remain the recipient of her exploration. Aggressive by nature, he knew he could take control of the situation at any moment, but her lack of experience and an unwelcome audience dissuaded him from succumbing to more volatile instincts.

Tension coiled within Libby as she sank deeper and deeper into an unfamiliar sensory world. Forced to trust her instincts, she prayed they would serve her well. Ever so slowly she traced the shape of Jake's lips and then the width of his mouth with the tip of her tongue. Shock held her immobile for an instant when she heart him groan low in his throat.

His fingers tightened slightly on the back of her neck, and she suddenly realized that he felt something more than indifference. Gripping the arms of her chair, Libby reminded herself that Jake Stratton was light-years out of reach, but that didn't prevent her from savoring the erotic brush of his mustache across her upper lip.

His lips parted, almost as if to provoke her curiosity. Libby didn't need coaxing. The courage flowering in her heart gave her the inspiration she needed to boldly explore the one man capable of reducing her to a muddled mass of sensations and desires.

The taste of him, dark and dangerous and so very male, nearly drove her mad. She trembled violently.

Jake instinctively responded to her arousal with his tongue darting forward to tangle lazily with hers. She sighed, the sound one of complete and utter capitulation, and as he had done the night before, he inhaled her essence into his own body.

Despite his hunger for Libby, Jake forced himself to pull back. He knew his body would soon betray him if he didn't, but he remained hunched over Libby in an effort to allow them both a moment to collect themselves.

She closed her eyes and tried to calm herself, regret and relief mingling within her. As her hold on the arms of her chair slowly eased, Libby rested her forehead against Jake's chin. She could hear the ragged sound of his breathing and knew that her own was just as uneven.

Reaching out, Jake cupped her cheek in his hand and waited for her to open her eyes. When she finally looked at him, he saw both disbelief and lingering desire.

"You remind me of the strawberries we had with breakfast," he whispered quietly. "So ripe, and so ready to eat."

She stared at him, mute with shock. He exhaled heavily and willed his body, which felt as thought it had been tied into a thousand small knots, to relax.

"You don't play fair, Professor."

Be careful, an inner voice warned. You're out of your league with this man. Libby ignored the warning. "I didn't know there were rules to this particular game."

Jake felt his body tighten in response to her challenge. "Shall I teach them to you?"

She hesitated, her desire for him at odds with her instinctive wariness. "I doubt I'd be a very good student."

"I'm an excellent—" Sounds exploded nearby, destroying the moment and Jake's patience.

He abruptly released a startled Libby, turned on his heel, and marched toward the growing chaos created by squawking birds fleeing the trees that formed the perimeter of the glade, rustling shrubbery, and the distinctive sound of human discomfort. Instinct and anger guided Jake, and he soon located the photographer he had hoped he wouldn't see until his return to Chicago.

He found the young man scrambling off an overpopulated anthill. Grabbing him by the collar of his jacket, Jake hauled him to his feet.

Brushing frantically at the army of ants clinging to his jeans and crawling up his torso, the photographer pleaded, "Help me, Mr. Stratton. They're all over me."

Jake ignored his distress. "That's your problem. You've broken our agreement. Our deal's off."

"But, Mr. Stratton—"

"You've got a lot of nerve," Jake interrupted angrily, "but you don't have an ounce of common sense. Hopefully you'll learn something from this experience. I will not have you dogging my every step. If you don't back off right now, I'll slap a restraining order on you that'll prevent you from getting within ten miles of me. I will then file charges of harassment. I may not be able to prove the charge, but I'll tie you up in court indefinitely. Are you getting my message?"

The young man hastily shed his jacket when he saw the ants working their way up his sleeves. "I didn't mean any harm."

"That's not the point, and you know it."

"But I quit *Celebrity Beat*!" he cried. "I'm on my own now."

Jake shook his head. "You've blown our deal. You'll have to take responsibility for the consequences of your actions."

He left the youthful photographer in the company of several thousand ants. Jake sincerely hoped the young man would locate his conscience in the very near future, but past experience with the media dimmed his optimism.

Five

Jake emerged from the forested area circling the glade. He began to relax as soon as he spotted Libby and realized that she intended to meet him halfway. His expression softened as he studied her relaxed smile. The look on his face effectively gentled the hard lines of his rugged features.

As they drew closer, he willingly discarded the tattered remnants of his anger. When measured against Libby, the young photographer ceased to be important. They stood facing each other a heartbeat later, both frozen in a moment of mutual observation and uncertainty.

Jake watched the breeze tug at her tresses and ruffle the hem of her jumper. He couldn't decide what he wanted to do more—bury his face in her silken mane or run his fingertips from her ankles to the tops of her thighs. Both, he decided. And repeatedly.

She watched him shove careless fingers through

the thick pelt of dark hair that fell across his forehead and also teased the collar of his jacket. She longed to test the density and texture of such a carelessly masculine hairstyle with her fingertips. Curious, too, about his broad chest, she suspected that a mat of equally dark and luxurious fur covered muscled flesh that would be searingly hot to the touch.

A wave of heat nearly toppled her. Libby took a steadying breath and tugged the shawl Jake had given her more snugly around her shoulders. Only the color in her cheeks betrayed the wayward nature of her thoughts.

"Is everything okay?" she finally asked.

Jake absently nodded, his thoughts straying again to those long legs she insisted on hiding beneath enough material to cover a wall of windows.

Frowning suddenly, he forced himself to reply to her question. "I think so. For the moment, anyway."

"Another photographer in hot pursuit of the entrepreneurial genius of the free world?" she teased when she saw his troubled expression.

He exhaled quietly, certain that she didn't understand how intrusive the media could be, and invariably would be if they spent any time together in public. "Unfortunately."

Jake glanced down at Libby in time to see the compassion in her eyes. Her reaction warmed him, and some of the isolation he felt lessened. Taking her hand, he led her to the edge of a low bluff that banked the northern side of Lake Hancock.

They walked in silence for several minutes.

When they reached the top of the bluff, they paused as if by mutual agreement. Whitecaps formed a quiltlike pattern across the width of the lake. The wind, colder and more forceful than in the sheltered glade, hinted that winter would soon arrive.

Jake stood behind Libby, briefly debating the wisdom of touching her until he simply gave in to the urge. He eased his arms down and around her waist. When she tensed, Jake knew he wouldn't force her to remain in his embrace. Prepared to release her, he experienced a moment of triumph when she sighed and allowed herself to relax against his sturdy body.

"What do you dream about, Libby?"

She twisted in his arms and glanced up at him, her surprise evident. "I don't dream." *I only have nightmares.*

He frowned. "Never?"

"Dreams are for children."

"Dreams are for everyone."

"No," she insisted as she returned her gaze to the choppy water of Lake Hancock. "They're not."

"Who destroyed your illusions, Libby?"

"It's impossible to have your illusions destroyed when you don't have any." She glanced at her watch. "We should get back to campus. Avery will be offended if we're late."

Jake anchored her against him when she tried to move out of his arms. "Don't run away from me," he ordered, his voice harsh, almost angry. "I promised you I wouldn't hurt you, and I meant it."

"You're not hurting me, Jake. You're simply reminding me of my priorities."

"Which are?"

"A full professorship," she answered honestly. "Tenure. My career at Hancock College means everything to me."

"There's more to life than being a slave to your work, Libby."

"I'm not a slave to anything. I am, however, committed to the goals I've set for myself."

Jake turned her around so that they faced each other. He saw a now-familiar blaze of anger flare in her eyes. The kindling heat within her also brought an added touch of color to her cheeks. Otherwise, she remained passive in posture and expression. He could feel her exerting the self-control she insisted on, and it infuriated him.

"What about a life away from your work? What about someone to care about? What about a family, children?"

Something precious and vulnerable inside her shattered, but Libby refused to betray the destructive results of Jake's hurtful questions. She kept her expression even, unaware that she exhibited the tension she felt in the white-knuckled grip she used to hold the shawl in place.

"What about children, Jake?"

His patience took an immediate dive into the lake. "Don't be obtuse. You know what I'm talking about."

"What I know is that you're being very rude. My private life is private. It stays that way."

"Dammit, Libby. Life isn't some endless treadmill. It's meant to be enjoyed, not simply endured."

She flinched. The look she gave him made Jake feel as though he'd struck her with his fist. She quickly fled his embrace. Feeling her absence deep in the marrow of his bones, he saw the forlorn expression on her face as she stared out across the lake and hugged herself for warmth as the wind molded her clothing to her slender figure.

Although she turned to confront Jake several moments later, Libby didn't really see him. Images of the past invaded her mind, images of a drunkard father who had turned her weak-willed mother into a fellow drunk and who invariably defended his cruelty and his excesses with the words, "Life's meant to be enjoyed, Libby girl. If there ain't any pleasure, then there ain't any reason to get up in the morning."

She shuddered and hugged herself even more tightly. She hated remembering the past, just as she'd learned to hate her father. Mick Kincaid represented the vile world she'd fled so long ago. She didn't know where he was, and she didn't care enough to find out. Knowing that he'd killed her mother in a drunken rage, and that he might one day decide to search out his daughter, was enough.

She blinked and brought Jake back into focus. "It's time to go. I appreciate . . . I enjoyed . . ." She hesitated, embarrassed by her verbal clumsiness. "Thank you for the picnic breakfast, Jake. It was lovely, but it's over now."

She started down the bluff's incline, but he reached out and caught her wrist. She didn't move a muscle when he positioned himself within a few inches of her shaking body and took her face in his hands.

"Are you all right?"

She nearly wept when she heard the concern in his voice. Yet another stone tumbled from the interior wall that held her together, and she grew panicky when she felt the foundation beneath that same wall start to shift under her. Libby scrambled mentally to regain her emotional footing.

Reaching up, she covered one of his hands with her own. "Thank you for your concern," she said, sincere despite her formal tone, "but I'm fine, Jake. Just think of me as a very realistic survivor. This might surprise you, but I'm quite content with the reality of my life."

Jake immediately targeted the most telling part of her remarks. "A survivor of what?"

"It doesn't matter."

"Yes, it does," he insisted as he vowed silently to have the whole truth from her one day.

Her chin wobbled. She bit her tongue to keep from admitting that fear of ending up in the same alcoholic cesspool occupied by her parents was the driving force behind her obsessive pursuit of professional success and economic security. Libby tightened the reins on her self-control. "Please. It's time to get back to campus."

Jake responded to her plea, but first he said, "I just want you to be happy."

The confusion in her eyes kept Jake from doing or saying anything more. He guided her from the bluff, across the glade, and into his car. Neither noticed the absence of their waiter and the festive patio tent, or the photographer who recorded their every move.

Settled in Jake's car, Libby reached into her leather satchel and found the file containing his agenda for the next six weeks. She handed it to him before he slipped the key into the ignition.

Jake's temper burst into life as he flipped through the multipage document. Laboring hard to restrain his fury, he tossed the file into Libby's lap and started the car.

She used the absence of conversation during the return trip to the Hancock campus as an opportunity to regain complete control over herself. After retrieving several hairpins from the bottom of her purse, Libby hastily scraped her hair into place and restored the tight bun at her nape. She then found her glasses, propped them on the bridge of her nose, and pretended to inspect the contents of the file folder Jake had tossed into her lap.

Libby kept reminding herself that he posed a very real threat to her very orderly life. Despite the repeated reminder, a little voice in her brain still urged her to take the risk and even welcome the affair Jake seemed determined to initiate between them. She tried to ignore the voice, but it refused to be silenced.

"You really want me out of your way, don't you?" he asked when he was fairly certain he wouldn't shout the question at her.

She couldn't bring herself to look at him. "You can always ask for an alternate liaison."

"We've had this conversation before, Libby."

Sighing, she kept her eyes on the file in her lap. "And I'm sure we'll have it again."

"You don't have a prayer of getting rid of me, so give it up. You're in the loop for the duration."

Libby decided to throw in the towel and admit that Jake Stratton was destined to go down in history as her first liaison-assignment failure. "It would be best if you have me replaced."

Jack gripped the steering wheel. "Not a chance, Professor, not a bloody chance in hell."

Libby felt the chill of Jake's aloofness all the way to Avery Mendenhall's office. She knew she couldn't fault Jake. She'd earned his anger. Nor could she fault his manners. He was unceasingly polite, which simply made her feel as though a gaggle of geese had decided to nibble on her nerves.

Delighted to have Jake on his academic turf, Avery apparently failed to notice Libby's strained expression or her silence as he launched into a discussion regarding the thrust of Jake's lecture series. He didn't even mention the fact that they'd arrived thirty minutes late for the meeting.

Libby almost appreciated being ignored. She struggled to use the time to deal with the emotional hunger Jake inspired in her heart, but she failed. The end of the two-hour meeting still found her lost in her own confused thoughts.

"Libby?" Avery said for the third time.

She glanced up to find the two men studying her with wide-ranging degrees of interest. Jake looked thoroughly bored, while the department chairman appeared bewildered to discover that she wasn't hanging on their every word.

She straightened in her chair. "Yes, Avery?"

"As I said a moment ago, the alumni luncheon begins in ten minutes."

"Of course." As she stood, she collected her leather satchel and purse. "We can leave now if you're ready, Mr. Stratton."

Jake nodded, but Libby saw the muscle ticking angrily in his strong jaw and the rigid set of his wide shoulders. She paled, but she made herself walk to the door despite Jake's obvious irritation with her formal manner.

She glanced back in time to see the two men shake hands and hear the department chair remind his guest lecturer, "If you have any problems at all, Jake, just let me know. We want you to enjoy yourself so much that you'll want to return in the very near future."

Jake followed Libby into the hall. "You forgot something." This time he didn't bother to drape the shawl over her shoulders. Instead, he simply shoved it into her hands as he walked by her. She very nearly wept as she walked at his side in silence.

Despite the palpable tension hovering between them, Libby's admiration and respect for Jake blossomed as the day unfolded. He charmed his admirers, and he disarmed those few skeptics who mistakenly assumed that his Tom Selleck looks and impressive physical attributes, rather than his intellect and business acumen, could somehow sustain him in the rough-and-tumble boardrooms of the international economic community or as a presidential adviser in the shark-infested waters of global politics.

Libby excused herself from the luncheon as soon as she introduced Jake to the host of the event. An hour and a half later she returned from teaching her freshman-level business communications class to find Jake in the process of accepting an award from the alumni association.

She paused inside the side-door entrance of the packed dining room. She knew she was being foolish, but she felt a burst of pride as she watched Jake at the podium. Tall, ruggedly handsome, and the epitome of gracious sophistication, he thanked the association for the award and then spoke eloquently on the topic of ethical business practices in the international business community.

Representatives of local and national TV networks, as well as several people in the audience, initiated an impromptu question-and-answer period as soon as Jake completed his remarks. He responded to their questions, skillfully sidestepping the intrusive ones regarding his love life while scanning the room for Libby.

She patiently waited for him to spot her. When he did, she lifted her wrist and pointed at her watch. Jake responded with a brusque nod, thanked everyone for their kindness, and slowly made his way in her direction.

About to compliment him on his award, Libby noticed the cold expression on his face as he walked past her and out of the building. She joined him, hurrying to keep up with his long-legged stride, but she confined her comments to a one-sentence explanation of the next stop on their campus tour.

A group of graduate students hijacked Jake as they left the luncheon, and he joined them in the student union for an impromptu exchange of ideas on the economic viability of Third World nations. While Jake spoke to the students, Libby found a phone and notified the head librarian of a possible delay, but they were only twenty minutes late for the scheduled book-signing and presentation of a hardbound copy of *Ethics in the Workplace* to the Hancock Library.

Libby knew Jake had spearheaded the fundraising effort for the library's new wing, so it didn't surprise her when Dean Cassidy, several department chairpersons, and the library staff willingly forgave him his tardiness. Once again, she silently congratulated him on his charismatic style.

A sorority tea followed, as did another TV interview when a reporter and his cameraman spotted Jake and Libby ducking out the back door of the administration building late that afternoon.

The next four days brought more of the same—a thoroughly hectic pace that forced Libby to juggle the schedule she'd designed for Jake, her teaching load, long hours each night working on her textbook, and the undeniable realization that she ached deep inside for the return of the man who had treated her with such tender concern as they stood on the bluff overlooking Lake Hancock.

Jake remained charming, articulate, and at ease with everyone. The woman at his side, however, felt invisible.

Libby endured each day by remaining in the background, asserting herself as a guide and clock-watcher only when necessary. She felt tremendous relief that Jake's lecture series would start the following Monday. She also felt drained by all the public appearances and social whirlwind required by Dean Cassidy and Avery Mendenhall.

She couldn't help wondering how Jake coped with this kind of thing on a daily basis.

Although she knew she should be grateful for Jake's indifferent behavior toward her, Libby quietly mourned the fact that her life had returned to normal. Normal as in boring, she amended regretfully as she watched him cope with a giggling group of coeds at yet another sorority tea.

Libby slipped out of the living room of the sorority house, her temples throbbing and her fatigue evident in the slump of her shoulders as she searched out a quiet spot. Although no closer to resolving her conflicted emotions, she didn't have the energy to deny her feelings any longer.

Four sleepless nights, and four days spent in the company of a man who made her hunger for love in the same way that she hungered for stability, forced Libby to confront the fact that she was on the brink of falling in love with Jake. As she fled the high-pitched laughter of the young women competing for his attention, she told herself that caring for Jake was impossible, insane, and unthinkable.

Certain that he wouldn't ever consider investing his emotions in a relationship, even a brief one, with a wallflower unsuited to his lifestyle, she summarily faulted his rugged features and powerful anatomy, his sense of humor, and his unsettling compassion.

Why had he let her see the real Jake Stratton? Did he simply pity her? she wondered bleakly. She loathed the idea of becoming his personal charity case. Anger sparked inside her, and Libby cursed his effortless seduction of, and subsequent encampment in, her heart.

Emotional need, however, threatened to eclipse both her anger and her fear of becoming a victim of her own desires. It also made her wonder if, in the final analysis, she possessed the identical genetic flaw capable of turning her into a mirror image of the weak-willed creature her mother had been. She hated the idea of becoming an emotional casualty, but she hated even more the prospect of never loving or being loved.

Jake found Libby leaning against the door of a coat closet beneath the central staircase of the sorority house. With her head bowed and her fingertips at her temples, her condition was obvious.

"I've had enough of all this, and so have you."

Libby straightened abruptly, her heart pounding so hard that she thought it might leap out of her chest at any moment. Before she could protest, Jake seized her arm and briskly escorted her out the door and to his car. He made short work of installing her in the passenger seat, fastening her seat belt, and then slamming the car door shut.

She started to speak, but the look he gave her as he slid into the driver's seat and buckled his own seat belt made her snap her mouth shut. "I mean it, Libby. I've had enough," he ground out between clenched teeth. "If you've got anything else on your blasted agenda, then cancel it. I'm finished performing for the entire population of Hancock, Illinois."

Fatigue and relief made her spontaneous. "Thank you."

Startled, he let the car engine idle. "Thank you?" he repeated. "For what?"

She smiled. "I needed a rescuer, and your timing was impeccable. Fortunately, there's nothing else on your agenda for today." Pausing, she opted for total candor. "And for the record, Jake, I'm tired of this circus too."

Her admission shocked him. He watched in amazement as she tugged the pins from her hair and released it from bondage. He watched in further amazement as she leaned back in her seat, closed her eyes, and groaned, "You don't have any aspirin, do you?"

Jake couldn't believe his eyes or his ears. "We'll find you some," he promised as he eased the car from the curb, joined the flow of traffic, and began his search for a drugstore. "But only if you'll stop doing that bun thing to your hair. I get a headache just looking at it."

She chuckled softly, amazed that she didn't feel the urge to smack him for his insulting cracks about her hairstyle. "We'll see, Jake."

Ten minutes later Libby downed two extra-strength aspirins as they sat in the parking lot of a fast-food restaurant sipping coffee. Feeling the same subdued pleasure she'd experienced during their unconventional picnic breakfast earlier in the week, she simply savored the moment and the man seated beside her.

"I owe you an apology."

She glanced at him in surprise. Her headache had already started to ease. "You do?"

He flashed a look in her direction guaranteed to scorch her nerve endings and give her an instant suntan all at once. "Of course I do. I've behaved like a total ass all week."

She shifted in her seat so that she could look at him more easily, and then risked a tentative smile. "Trained seal might be a better description."

He grinned at her. Reaching out for her free hand, he laced their fingers together. He kept his thumb on a pulse point in her slender wrist. Moments later, he experienced a surge of satisfaction when he felt the wildly throbbing evidence of her reaction to him.

Libby tried to keep their conversation as businesslike as possible, despite the pervasive warmth of his skin. "How do you cope with the constant performance pressure, Jake? I'd go nuts if people kept shoving microphones under my nose."

His grin and his satisfaction faded. "The same way you cope with me. I just try to tune it out until I can't stand it any longer. Then I make a break for the nearest exit."

She paled. "I don't tune you out."

His gaze narrowed. "Don't you?"

"Of course not!" she exclaimed, although she knew she was lying to herself and to him. "I simply try to stay out of your way and do my job."

"You're avoiding the real issue here, aren't you?"

Too flustered to admit that he was right, she insisted, "I don't know what you're talking about."

He leaned toward her and relieved her of her now-empty plastic coffee cup. Libby instinctively began to edge back toward the door, but Jake froze her in place with his piercing gray eyes.

"You know what the bottom line here is? I got too close, and you freaked. You found clothes in the back of your closet a corpse wouldn't wear, you designed a schedule guaranteed to eliminate anything but basic amenities between us, and then you retreated behind a veil of silence suitable for a Middle Eastern woman. I added insult to injury by letting you get away with this stunt, and we've both been on edge all week, but I'm not giving up on you, Libby. I've got more staying power and more stubbornness than anyone I know—even you—so I'll wait you out if that's what's necessary."

His criticism, some of it painfully on target, stung, but she nonetheless felt abandoned when he released her hand and shifted back into his bucket seat. She watched him take hold of the steering wheel with both hands, and she wondered if it would bend under his fierce grip.

"Jake, the last thing I want to do is offend you," she began with as much tact as she could muster.

"Damnit, don't act like I'll try to have you fired because I can't get you into my bed. Sexual harassment isn't my style."

"I didn't mean to imply that it was," she pointed out, primarily because questioning Jake's integrity hadn't even occurred to her. She knew better than to question it now. "It's just that we don't have anything in common. Our lifestyles and our worlds clash, so it's best not to become . . . overly personal."

"We're attracted to each other, and you're fighting the inevitable."

"Nothing's inevitable," she disagreed, although she didn't deny that her feelings went beyond simply finding him attractive. "Jake, I just don't know how to be casual and worldly with a man like you. And even though I might be tempted to try, for me it would be like standing out in the middle of a busy intersection and inviting a hit-and-run accident."

A man like you. The words reverberated in his head. He didn't know how to react, so he held his emotions in check and calmly said, "I'm not asking you to commit suicide. I'm just asking for a little trust. I promised you I wouldn't hurt you. I meant it."

Her expression softened. "You wouldn't mean to, but that's what would happen. I'm not like your women, Jake. I'm different. I don't know the rules, and I don't want to learn them. I just can't risk it, not even for you."

He studied her for several silent minutes. Libby felt his tension and his frustration. She also felt a profound sense of loss.

"You *are* different, Libby." *And that's why I can't even consider walking away from you,* he finished silently. Libby, he realized, had become far more than a challenge in a very short time.

She remained quiet as he started the car, put it in gear, and exited the parking lot. "Shall I drop you at your place and then pick you up in the morning, or would you rather go to the hotel so you can get your car?"

"The hotel, please," she said as she kept her gaze on the heavy Friday evening traffic. "The weekend is all yours unless you want to attend the Panther game at the stadium. Dean Cassidy has a private box you can use. You might also want to drop in on the glee club's Sunday afternoon concert at the performing-arts center."

"Thanks, but I'll pass. I'd just as soon keep a low profile."

"All right," she said so softly that Jake almost didn't hear her. A quick glance in her direction told him absolutely nothing about her state of mind.

Five minutes later Jake watched Libby drive out of the hotel parking lot. As he handed his car keys to the parking attendant and made his way into the hotel lobby, he promised himself that he wouldn't give up on Libby.

Jake knew he had to find a way to come to terms with his gnawing hunger for a real personal life. He missed the days, if not the poverty, when he called his life his own. And he felt a deep longing for someone willing to share both the good and the bad aspects of the notoriety and visibility his success had spawned.

Jake sensed that Libby could be that someone.

Six

Satisfied with the end notes she'd written for Chapter 21 of her textbook, Libby pressed the computer keyboard's "save" key. She decided that she would do a final edit on the material in the morning and then begin the end notes for the next chapter. With a little luck she might be able to complete the task before lunch.

Removing her glasses, Libby placed them atop a stack of reference books beside the computer. She leaned back in her chair, lifted her arms, and stretched to loosen the tension that had crept into her back and neck during the previous five hours.

The door chime sounded as she brought her arms down and exhaled heavily. Libby glanced at her watch, noted the hour, and then made her way to the front door. She assumed Clarice Martin, her neighbor, had noticed her glowing porch light and had decided to stop in following her shift as a dispatcher at the Hancock Police Department.

Libby pulled open the door, a smile on her face. "No lectures about opening my door to strangers, Clarice. You're as regular as clock—" Her smile slipped a few notches. "You're not Clarice."

Jake inspected himself to be sure. "Not this week, anyway," he confirmed with a grin.

Surprise made her abrupt. "What's wrong? What are you doing here?"

He shrugged, the gesture far more casual than Jake actually felt. He should have known better than to just show up on her doorstep, but as he studied her now, he knew that this was exactly where he wanted—and needed—to be.

"I saw your light," he said as he took in the pale cream jogging outfit she wore, her bare feet, and the unbound glory of her long hair. Like an endless waterfall cascading across her shoulders and down her back, it prompted a tumult of erotic images that had an immediate and profound effect on him.

Libby peered past him, squinting slightly in order to see the curb at the end of the sidewalk. Jake knew what she was looking for.

"I've been out walking."

"But your hotel's at least five miles from here."

He nodded. "I guess I didn't really notice the distance."

Still poised in the doorway, Libby grappled with her uncertainty. Torn between inviting him into her home and sending him on his way, she asked, "Is there something wrong?"

"Not really. Walking helps me clear my head after I've worked too many eighteen-hour days."

Would you like to come in? hovered on the tip of

her tongue, but she shied away from actually issuing the invitation.

"Did you get a chance to look at those lesson plans I gave you for the lecture series?" Wonderful! she thought disgustedly. Impress the man with your snappy repartee.

"That's what I've been doing since I got back to the hotel. I thought we could go over them this weekend, if you have time."

Bend a little, Libby, and invite me in despite the fact that it's nearly midnight.

As if reading his mind, she noted, "It's awfully late."

"I've always been a night owl." He looked past her and saw the stack of open reference books and the blinking cursor light on the computer screen. "I guess we both are. You're working, aren't you? I suppose you want to get back to it."

Don't keep pushing me away, Libby.

She reached out when he started to step back, thought better of her spontaneity, and quickly withdrew her hand. "Don't leave, Jake. I'm finished for the night." Taking a deep breath, she willed her heart to a slower pace and stepped out of his way. "I've been at the computer since I got home."

"Any hot cocoa on the stove?"

She smiled, recalling their first evening together as she closed the door and followed him into the combination living room and dining area. Unwilling and unable to ignore his bold stride, she realized that Jake walked into a room as though he already owned it. While she envied his unflagging confidence, she also craved the sensitivity and passion that seemed second nature to him.

She couldn't take her eyes off him. His attire, so typically Jake, announced disregard for the conservative image projected by most businessmen. She liked the vertical black-and-white awning-style stripes of his shirt, the sleeves rolled up to reveal powerful forearms, and the unbuttoned collar that exposed his tanned throat and neck. Nor did she find fault with the tailored cut of black trousers that emphasized his narrow hips, sturdy legs, and the generous endowment that made him undeniably male.

While her heart thunked around in her chest like a wrecking ball, Libby forced her gaze to floor level. She almost groaned when she realized that she even liked his leather loafers.

Face it, she told herself, there isn't anything you *don't* like about this man.

"No hot cocoa?" Jake asked a second time, a curious expression on his face when he saw Libby's bewildered look and flushed cheeks. "You okay?"

She squared her shoulders and discarded her reckless thoughts. At least, she tried to. "I'm fine. I do have some cold beer."

Jake paused in the middle of the large room as she spoke. The pale mauves and sandstones of the desert Southwest decor of Libby's home immediately confirmed his belief that she possessed a quietly elegant sense of style. Yet again, he wondered about her reluctance to translate that style to her wardrobe.

"Planning a wild party?" he asked on a teasing note.

"What do you think?" she asked with a laugh, striving for a nonchalance she didn't feel as she walked to her desk and turned off the computer.

Pausing beside the chair, she watched him inspect the home she had created for herself. She wondered if he could even begin to understand how precious the environment was to her. Her books, which occupied an entire wall of floor-to-ceiling shelves, the collection of charcoal sketches of Lake Hancock by an obscure but talented local artist that she'd matted and framed herself, the furniture she'd found at garage sales and then refinished and recovered, and the now-abundant ferns she'd nurtured from seedlings, all represented her childhood dream of a real home.

Libby frowned for a long moment. She realized that her fear of placing a loved one in jeopardy had prevented her from including another person in her dream of the perfect home. Jake reminded her, more than any man she'd ever known, of the absence of someone to love in her life.

"I like your home."

His comment chased away her melancholy thoughts and lessened her inner tension. She smiled suddenly, and her face glowed with the brightness of a brilliant midday sun. "Me too. In fact, it's one of my favorite places."

Delighted that he'd finally said the right thing, Jake strolled toward the kitchen. Libby followed him. She didn't protest when he opened the refrigerator and located one of the long-necked bottles of German beer she'd recently purchased—for him.

After rifling through two utility drawers, she found what she needed.

"Are you hungry?" she asked as she handed him a bottle opener. His fingers brushed over hers, and her heart sang.

"No, but thanks for asking." He removed the top and took a long swig of beer straight from the bottle.

Libby silently cursed her own thoughtlessness, as well as the absence in her life of caring parents inclined to teach her the correct social graces. "I've got plenty of glasses."

"No need. It'll spoil the taste."

Bemused, she said, "Oh."

Jake smiled easily and moved out of the way so that she could precede him down the short hallway. The seductive swaying of her long hair mesmerized and aroused him. Pausing behind one of the dining-room chairs, more out of necessity than curiosity, Jake glanced at Libby when he saw the reference material, numerous chubby files, notepads, and manuscript pages stacked tidily on the dining-room table.

"My first textbook," she confirmed.

"That's what I thought." Jake noted, and approved of the quiet pride her heard in her voice. "By the look of things, you're almost finished with it."

"Another fifty pages of text, plus the chapter end notes, and I'll have the first draft completed." She didn't say anything more, primarily because she didn't want him to know that she would've been done with the rough draft by now had it not been for her assignment as his liaison person.

Libby waited until he sat down on the couch before finding a seat in a comfortable chair opposite him, all the while pondering the wisdom of confronting him about his arrival on her doorstep so late at night. She felt compelled to understand his motives. She also wanted to know why he seemed interested in her and her relatively miniscule—when measured against the global concerns he dealt with on a daily basis—slice of the world.

"I'm surprised to see you, Jake."

"You shouldn't be."

"After our conversation this afternoon, I thought you—"

"Might be angry," he finished for her as he placed the beer bottle on the coffee table in front of him and leaned back against overstuffed pillows.

She shifted uneasily in her chair. "Perhaps."

"Why would I be angry, Libby?"

She sensed he wasn't being facetious or flip, so she quietly pointed out, "I didn't say what you wanted to hear. Most people are offended when you won't give them what they want."

"I'm not most people." Jake abandoned his relaxed pose and leaned forward so that his elbows rested on his powerful thighs, his expression startlingly serious. "Libby, you spoke your mind. Candor isn't a quality I dislike or reject, so how can I fault you for your honesty? It's something I've learned to expect and count on from you."

"Even when I say things you really don't want to hear?"

He smiled, but Libby missed the teasing glimmer normally evident in his thickly lashed gray eyes. He looked . . . lonely, she realized with surprise.

"Even then, Professor."

"You're different," she whispered, finally believing what her heart had been trying to tell her since their first meeting.

"We both are, Libby."

She laced her fingers together in her lap and then studied the tangled weave before looking at him. In the soft light and subtle color scheme of the room, Jake seemed larger than life to her. In many ways, she realized, he was. The fact that he exuded power in the same way that other men exuded fear when faced with their own mortality simply drove the point of his uniqueness home to her.

Lifting her chin and marshaling her courage, she gave him a steady look. "The few men I've dated haven't ever been willing to see my point of view. They didn't understand my reluctance to become involved in a casual relationship or to indulge in even more casual sex, and they didn't come back when I refused to sleep with them."

"That's their loss, Libby, and very definitely my gain, because I don't intend to stop coming back. And for the record, when we *make love*, it won't be casual," Jake assured her emphatically. "It will, however, be intense, overwhelming, and thoroughly devastating."

She went very still, so still that she resembled an exquisitely fragile sculpture. "Is that why you're here now, Jake?"

The door chime sounded once again, providing additional punctuation to her breathless question. Libby somehow found the strength to leave her chair and make her way to the front door. Her inquiry remained unanswered, her emotions in total disarray.

Given the shock in her enormous blue eyes and the late hour, Jake followed her. "Busy place you've got here," he noted as he silently cursed the untimely interruption.

Still reeling from Jake's frank remark, Libby glanced over her shoulder as she fumbled for the door latch. "It's just Clarice. She stops by after work if she sees my front light on."

Jake wondered if she was right.

Unfortunately she wasn't.

Libby's smile froze when a man lunged forward and a flash of light exploded in her face. Momentarily blinded, she turned in confusion and crashed into Jake's broad chest. He jerked her against him and muttered a thoroughly obscene word as he tried to shield his eyes with his free hand.

On the verge of uttering some pretty ugly things herself, Libby blinked rapidly and tried to keep her face averted as several additional flashes of light blazed in the semidark entryway. She struggled to free herself and reach the porch light switch, but Jake held her tightly and maneuvered her backward into the living room. She stumbled over the edge of a throw rug despite his firm hold, but he kept her upright and moving.

Feeling invaded and violated, she twisted in Jake's arms as she tried to see the photographer. She squinted against the flashing light as the man pursued them. Her impaired vision provided a star-studded image of a small figure dressed in black who wielded his camera like a weapon.

Although shaken by the behavior of the man, Libby found her voice and ordered, "Get out of my home right now, or I'll call the police."

Angrier than he'd been in many years, Jake shoved Libby into a chair. "Stay put."

She grabbed his hand. "Be careful."

He squeezed her fingers and then advanced on the photographer, naked fury in his eyes. The young man quickly turned tail and ran for the door. Jake sprinted after him, charging out the open front door, across the porch, down the stairs, and out onto the sidewalk. But he skidded to a stop at the edge of the curb as the photographer ducked into the open passenger door of a waiting vehicle that quickly sped off into the night.

The sound of squealing tires aroused a noisy chorus of protest from the dogs in the neighborhood. The acrid smell of burning rubber crystallized Jake's growing desire for a lifestyle that didn't include being hounded by irresponsible members of the press for the rest of his natural life.

Jake uttered another oath as he made his way back into Libby's house. He blamed himself for the photographer's invasion of her privacy. Wanting her, he realized bleakly, didn't justify exposing her to the harsh glare of public scrutiny or the embarrassment he was certain she would feel once the photos of them in an awkward clinch hit the local newsstands.

He paused just inside the living room, disgust and frustration hardening his already rugged features. He consciously searched out the inner calm that he tapped into when under pressure, but the street fighter in him, the boy who'd survived the uglier streets of Chicago during his childhood, resisted his effort. Certain that Libby would be upset about what had just occurred, Jake didn't quite know how to react to the expression on her face.

She stood in the middle of the living room, her initial uncertainty displaced by her compassion for Jake when she saw his grim look and tense body. Feeling an overwhelming need to lighten his mood and to reassure him that she didn't hold the photographer's behavior against him, she decided to trust her instincts.

"All this attention," she remarked teasingly, "just because you're giving graduate-level lectures at Hancock College. I don't think the dean had any idea of just how popular you are with the press." She took a step toward him. "I shudder to think what those crazy people do to you when you go out for pizza. And that photographer. He certainly can't get enough of you, can he?"

Jake warned, "They can't get enough of *us*, Libby. You're going to be front-page news in some sleazy tabloid one of these days, so prepare yourself. It won't be pleasant for you."

She laughed, the sound spontaneous and filled with disbelief. "When they realize I'm not anyone important, they'll just paste in a picture of some glamorous woman you already know. If you're worried about me, Jake, please don't be. Trust me, you'll laugh about this tomorrow."

Jake closed the distance between them and tugged her into his arms. He savored her desire to reassure him, but he knew she lacked the street smarts and sophistication of the women he usually dated. Amazed, too, by her innocent generosity, he studied her uplifted face and silently promised himself that he would protect her from her lack of experience. He knew it wouldn't be long before the photos were published and others discovered her unsophisticated beauty.

"I know you believe what you're saying, Libby, but this type of thing can get out control very quickly. I don't want you embarrassed or hurt by it."

Charmed by what she considered needless worry, she smiled up at him. She liked the security and comfort she found in his embrace, and she especially liked the feel of his hands pressing against the small of her back.

The heat of him warmed her, inside and out. The essence of this man, so powerful, so intense, called out to her in a thoroughly compelling way, and she never wanted to leave his arms.

"I'll schedule a press conference," Jake announced. "The sooner I deal with these people, the better."

"If you think it's necessary," she agreed as she basked in the heady rush of emotions prompted simultaneously by his concern for her and the heat stealing into her bloodstream. "It might be awkward if they start popping up in the classroom. Neither you nor the students deserve that kind of interruption when you're lecturing."

He nodded, his attention shifting abruptly to the brilliant blue of her large eyes, the translucence of her fair skin, and the almost dreamy look in her eyes. He reacted immediately to Libby, the volatile quality of his rising desire overcoming the control he normally maintained over his body and his emotions.

Libby's eyes widened when she felt the change in him, but she couldn't bring herself to pull away. She trembled, and her eyelids drifted closed as Jake leaned down. The world disappeared. She moaned softly, the sound more erotic and stimulating than she realized. Set adrift in a tumultuous sea of sensation the instant Jake claimed her lips, she opened to him, welcoming him with a breathless willingness that shocked them both.

Need shuddered through every inch of Jake's body as their tongues tangled in a wild mating ritual that made her throw caution to the far winds and embrace the reckless desire coursing through her. When Jake lowered his hands and snugged her more firmly against his lower body, Libby willingly cradled his potent strength and acknowledged his desire by curling into him like a swirl of liquid heat.

She clearly understood words like "bereft" and "abandoned" when Jake jerked free of her and threw back his head a few minutes later. She listened, as though from a great distance, to his ragged breathing as it competed with her own struggle for oxygen. She sagged against him, but he soon clasped her face between his palms and gently tilted her head upright so that he could see her expression.

"Open your eyes and look at me, Libby."

Too overwhelmed by the raging storm within,

she didn't protest his rough-voiced demand. She simply complied.

They stared at each other, both stunned, both hungry for more, and both struggling for some remnant of reason in the wake of their passion for one another.

"You asked me an important question a little while ago, but I never got a chance to answer you. I want to now."

She nodded, because she remembered the question, too, and she wanted an answer. She no longer doubted that he would tell her the truth, but she wondered if she could live with it.

"You asked me if I came here tonight to make love to you. I didn't. I showed up on your doorstep because this is where I needed to be."

Need. She mulled the word over in her mind for a few moments. She discovered that she disliked it. "Then any woman . . ." she began.

"No," he interrupted sharply. "Just any woman will not do. I need *you*, Libby."

"Why?" she asked in a small voice that sounded strained. "I don't understand."

"I see in you what no one else seems to see. I know what you're hiding, Libby. If you'll let me, I'll show you."

Alarmed, she insisted, "But I'm not hiding anything."

He smiled at her very tenderly. "You're hiding yourself. You've managed to hide your warmth, your gentleness, your compassion, your femininity, and your intelligence for God only knows how long. I can't let you do that anymore."

"That's crazy." She twisted out of his arms,

unnerved that he'd spotted the deception that had worked with everyone else. "I'm nothing like your women, Jake. You're rationalizing your presence here."

He frowned briefly, but he concealed his frustration with her denial of the truth behind a reasonable tone of voice. "Despite what you and the rest of the world seem to think, I don't keep a harem at my beck and call. Yes, I have a number of women friends, but they're just friends. I haven't been involved with anyone in a very long time. Intimacy means too much to me to abuse it with careless sex."

She flushed. "I just assumed that you . . . get around," she finished apologetically.

He exhaled, the sound heavy with frustration. "Apparently everyone *assumes*, whether or not it's true."

"Why, Jake? Just tell me the real reason. If you're honest, I can find a way to live with the results." She hoped she wasn't lying to herself.

He caught her hands and pulled her against his hard body. She groaned at the searing contact and drew in a shattered breath. Jake, his nerve endings nearing a meltdown, shuddered.

"I want you," he said, a fierceness in his voice that even he didn't recognize. "It's that simple."

"We're both old enough," she whispered, "to know that life isn't simple. It's complicated, it's often lonely, and sometimes it's frightening."

"You told me you weren't afraid of me."

She stiffened, but in the end she admitted the truth. "What I feel for you frightens me."

He pressed her cheek to his chest and held her

tightly, all the while wanting to strike back at the person responsible for her fear. "Who hurt you?" he asked.

She shifted backward and looked up at him. *No one hurt me. I've never let anyone that close.* Although she couldn't say the words aloud, her eyes tried to tell him that he alone had the power to destroy her.

"Will you let me show you how much I want you?"

"And after you show me?"

He wanted to say that he had no intention of leaving her, but he sensed she wouldn't believe him. Instead, he released her and promised himself that the choice of how to proceed was totally up to Libby.

"We'll decide that together," he vowed.

She wrestled with his honesty for a moment, and she repaid him by being honest with herself. Even if Jake didn't love her, and even though he would leave her behind at the end of his lecture series, she wanted him now.

Libby extended her hand, her clear-eyed expression and the determination evident in her posture a statement of her intent. Jake reached out too. Their fingers tangled. The air around them seemed charged with currents of expectation.

"I don't expect or want any promises of undying love, Jake. I do want what happens between us to be totally honest at all times."

"No expectations, no disappointments?"

She half smiled at the cliché, despite the potentially hurtful meaning inherent in the phrase and the chagrin in his voice. "Exactly."

She led him down a short hallway, but she paused in the doorway of her bedroom. Looking up at him, she felt warmth and security when she saw the intensity of his expression as he studied her.

Libby moved forward alone. She paused near the brass bed that dominated a bedroom of soft mauves and burgundies. Pivoting, she faced him and quietly said, "Please make love to me, Jake."

Seven

The instant she finished speaking, Libby knew that the final stone of the wall protecting her heart had tumbled free. Supremely vulnerable, but still aching with desire for Jake, she felt a nagging sense of uneasiness about her ability as a lover.

Despite that feeling, she remained standing in the center of the room, breathless with anticipation and bathed in the soft glow of light provided by the small lamps located on the nightstands on either side of her bed. She felt Jake's eyes on her. Her heartbeat sped up. Trembling like a willow caressed by a gentle summer breeze, Libby awaited the touch she had dreamed about every night and every day since their first meeting.

Pride and relief exploded in Jake's chest as he approached her. Pride that she had found the courage to express her need, and profound relief that she had chosen him to receive her trust. He raised a shaking hand and traced the curve of her cheek with his fingertips. Using his other hand, he slowly lowered the zipper of the jacket of her jogging outfit.

The air moving in and out of Jake's lungs halted abruptly when he saw her bare skin. He blinked, her nakedness beneath the jacket a shock and an eloquent promise of things to come. Hunger for Libby raged inside him, but he forced himself to hold back. He longed to make their first time together an experience she would never regret.

He gazed at her face. Instead of the uncertainty he expected to see, Jake discovered a surprising blend of serenity and desire shining in her eyes. Just minutes before he'd worried about her poorly concealed anxiety at the prospect of intimacy, but she now appeared ready to welcome him into her arms and her body without restraint and without hesitation. He paused, struggling to grasp the transformation now taking place in her.

Unwilling to be denied because of her own inexperience, Libby began to trust instincts rooted deep within her. Shrugging free of her jacket, she let it drift to the floor. She heard Jake's swift intake of breath and registered the disbelief in his eyes when she took his hands and lifted them to her full, high breasts.

She gasped softly. Her head fell back, and her eyes fluttered closed for a moment as she absorbed the shock of the scorching contact. Covering his hands with her own, Libby pressed them against her aching flesh, all those years of denial and mistrust relegated to the past for now.

She moaned, the sensual sound beginning low in her throat. Nothing in her life had prepared her for this moment, or for the devastating knowledge that she was being touched by the man she had already begun to love.

"I didn't know I could feel this way," she whispered in a shattered little voice that nearly destroyed Jake's self-control.

Her breasts swelled and firmed, filling his hands with unanticipated bounty. Her nipples tightened and stabbed gently at his palms. Silky and hot to the touch, her skin felt like a blazing inferno.

Jake's heartbeat thundered in his ears. She moaned yet again, the sound raw, very nearly primitive.

"Libby," he breathed, his voice ragged and filled with an awe brought on by her actions and her courage. "Touching you is like having the sun in my hands."

She whispered, "I've never wanted anyone else to touch me this way."

"Are you absolutely certain this is what you want?" he forced himself to ask.

She opened her eyes and met his serious gaze in the mirror. She glanced briefly at his hands, which overflowed with her throbbing flesh. Despite the enormity of the step they were about to take, she knew beyond a doubt that she was exactly where she wanted—and needed—to be.

"I think I'd die if we stopped now."

Unprepared for her candid admission, Jake felt a fire storm streak through his bloodstream. She called out to him on every level imaginable.

She evoked raw hunger, she promised emotional fulfillment. She roused every protective inclination he had ever harbored, and her gentle nature appeased the stark demand of a heart desperate for warmth and love. She answered pleas not yet verbalized, and then she provoked additional ones.

He slowly slid his hands up her torso, traced her delicate collarbone with his fingertips, and then cupped her slender shoulders. Turning her so that she faced the mirrored sliding doors of the closet that covered an entire wall in her bedroom, Jake forced her to confront the reality of their actions.

She stared at their reflections, her gaze immediately drawn to Jake's taut facial features. She felt his tension, but she also sensed unnamed pain deep inside him. She suddenly wanted to comfort him, but when she tried to turn in his arms, he held her still with a firm grip on her waist. He remained positioned behind her.

"Jake?"

"Look at yourself, Libby. How could I not want you? How could any normal man not want you?"

She reluctantly did as he demanded. She looked at herself, and she saw a woman naked to the waist. A woman whose breasts ached almost painfully and whose nipples needed the wet heat of Jake's mouth around them. Flushed with desire, she finally noticed the movement of his hands.

Fascinated, she watched him briefly span her narrow waist before he skimmed his fingertips up her taut midriff. When he cupped her full breasts in his hands, she experienced a sudden spark of wholly feminine pride deep inside. Although she hadn't appreciated the abundance of her hourglass-shaped figure in the past, she now did.

"You're exquisite, Libby," he told her as he leaned down and nuzzled her neck.

Raising her arms, she arched languidly and brought her hands together at the back of his neck. The movement made her breasts jut forward with invitation. She didn't recognize herself any longer. Jake's fingers contracted, sending a flutter of sensation directly to her womb.

She held on to him as though her life depended upon the strength of her grasp. Feeling the seductive pull of his touch, her body tensed and then trembled as he savored the weight of her breasts with his hands and stroked her nipples to burning points of desire with his fingertips.

"Please, Jake," she begged, even though she didn't know what she needed or wanted.

He circled around her and dropped to his knees in front of her, his lips sipping at her breasts, his fingers tracing trails of sensation up and down her spine. She watched him, stunned by the feel of his tongue and teeth at her nipples and the sensations provoked by his touch.

The erotic image of their bodies reflected in the mirror robbed her of breath and weakened her knees. Heat flared between her legs. Nothing, not even her wildest fantasies, had prepared her for the devastation she now experienced.

Feeling suddenly light-headed, she gripped his shoulders for balance. Her long hair matched the forward sway of her body, flowing across her shoulders and tumbling over her breasts in an erotic cascade.

Jake slipped his hands inside the waistband of her slacks and slowly inched them down past the gentle swell of her hips. He kept his gaze on her, observing even the subtlest of her reactions.

He felt her tremble violently. But the look of need on her face eased his worry that he might be moving too fast for her. Her slacks slid free to pool at her ankles. The skimpy lace panties she wore proved an inadequate barrier to his questing fingers.

He hugged her close, the lushness of her shapely body so arousing that he fought for control as he pressed his face to the valley between her breasts and inhaled the scent of her skin. Before too long he brought himself back under control and began to conduct shattering little forays up and down her bare thighs with his fingertips, the small sounds of breathless disbelief coming from Libby making it almost impossible for him to stop.

"Let me touch you too," she whispered urgently.

Her soft words eventually brought him to his feet. He stood very still, towering over her as he allowed her the luxury of exploration. He discovered an untapped well of patience inside himself as she fumbled with the buttons of his shirt, finally freeing them all and peeling the fabric from his body.

He even withstood the erotic torture of Libby sinking her fingers into the thick pelt of hair covering his chest. But he couldn't stifle the groan that escaped him when she touched his nipples, coaxed them to hard buds, and then pressed hot kisses to each one.

He suddenly tunneled his fingers through her hair and bracketed her head between his strong hands, his fear of frightening Libby eclipsed by the driving force of his need. He watched her eyes drift closed. He felt her fingers tangle in the dense hair of his chest.

Her chin rose slowly, her head tilting back into his hands. She conveyed her trust in him and her pleasure that he had claimed her for himself without words, but Jake immediately understood. Leaning down, he sampled the tender skin of her throat with his tongue, her delicate shudder confirmation that he'd correctly responded to her unspoken message.

Lifting his head, his senses filled with the taste and honeysuckle scent of her warm skin, he watched her intently, his eyes dangerous and dark with arousal and his heart filled with emotions he couldn't even begin to name. Libby embodied every erotic thought he'd ever had or would have. Desperate for her touch, he guided her hands to his belt, but he left the final choice up to her.

Libby responded instantly, but not only to Jake's expectations. She knew exactly what she wanted. Despite the clumsiness of her fingers, she unfastened the belt, freed the button, and then lowered the zipper of Jake's trousers. Tugging his briefs and trousers past his hips, she ran her fingertips up and down the backs of his muscled thighs before sliding her hands forward to the front of his body.

Desire and the rigid shaft nudging her lower abdomen emboldened her, and she explored him even more intimately with her fingertips. Looking up, she saw his tight jaw and the strain etching his features as she clasped the hard, hot strength of his sex between her hands. He shuddered, and she smiled up at him—a slow, sweet, and very erotic smile of a temptress.

Heat simmered within her. She could feel the part of her body that would soon welcome him begin to throb and moisten in anticipation as she stroked and fondled him.

Jake's control snapped without warning. He seized Libby and jerked her up against his hard body. His mouth descended like an avenging angel. His tongue invaded her mouth, and he greedily staked his claim on every crevice and ridge within.

Cradling her hips in his hands, he snugged her pelvis against the steel-hard evidence of his desire, and then taunted her with a grinding pressure that nearly sent him reeling into oblivion.

Libby reacted instantly, insatiable in her hunger for him. Her restraint disappeared. Any fear lurking in the recesses of her consciousness vanished. Libby surrendered, a willing hostage, an adept student.

Their tongues dueled with passionate intent. They simultaneously reached out for each other, feverishly touching, stroking, and arousing to the point of pain. Neither held anything back.

Urgency prevailed. They did not pause. They could not pause, even when they were both panting and straining for air.

Hurling themselves forward, they seemed intent on pushing each other beyond the brink of sanity and into the arms of sensual madness.

Jake wrenched his mouth from her lips; he had no choice. He gasped for air. His heart seemed ready to burst out of his chest, his body out of control.

She clung to him, shattered and shaking. "Don't stop," she gasped. "Don't stop now."

Air gusted harshly in and out of his lungs as he kicked free of his clothing and lifted her up against his body. "I won't take you on the floor."

"Doesn't matter," she insisted frantically. "It doesn't matter."

She wrapped her legs around his hips and repeatedly thrust against him. Jake almost dropped her, but he managed to carry her to the bed. Sprawled beside her a heartbeat later, he tugged her back into his arms and held her.

"It does matter. I'm too close to the edge." He claimed her mouth in a quick, searing kiss. "I don't want to hurt you."

"I won't break," she wailed, so out of control that she didn't care how she sounded.

He smoothed back the tangled strands of her hair that clung to her flushed cheeks. "You don't know how close I am to losing it."

The look she gave him made his nerve endings sizzle. "Then lose it . . . inside me."

Submerged in the dense silk of her long hair, his fingers clenched. His eyes darkened, and his anatomy hardened to satin-covered granite. "I plan to," he promised in a low voice fraught with tension.

She reached out and quickly found his arousal. His body jerked at the contact, and she gloried in the hard, hot, and incredibly smooth ridge of flesh caught between her hands. She felt her nipples tingle and tighten, and a shiver traveled from the top of her head to the tip of her toes.

"I want you," she told him brazenly as she rolled flush against him. "Now."

"I'm on fire for you, too, but I want to protect you."

"No need."

He stopped her busy hands for a moment and eased her back against the pillows. He loomed over her, his entire body on fire and his nerves thoroughly tattered. "Why not?"

She groaned in frustration. "Trust *me*, Jake. I'm not a fool."

"You're anything but, my love."

She stroked him when he freed her hands. Her hips moved in erotic counterpoint to the motion of her hands. She moaned when Jake leaned down and found the tip of one of her breasts with his lips. His fingers glided down her flat belly and then dipped into the tangled silk and wet heat at the top of her thighs. Libby arched up off the bed with a cry akin to pain, her body quivering and her head thrashing against the pillow.

Heat exploded between them once again, but this time a conflagration ensued.

Jake followed his fingertips with his lips. He bit at her skin and then soothed the tiny bites with openmouthed kisses that left a trail of sensual torment in their wake.

Gasping for air, Libby felt the mattress shift under her as Jake situated herself between her thighs. She clutched at the quilt as he stroked her and murmured tender words.

Eyes closed, air rasping in and out of her lungs, and neck arched, she went wild when his mouth settled over her weeping flesh. Frenzied sensation rushed through her entire body. She came completely apart, a willing victim to Jake's pleasurable torture of her body.

He moved up over her before she recovered. Thrusting into her, he sank into her inner fire. Her body closed around him, saturating him with wet flames and obliterating any self-control he might have once possessed. He gathered her against him, his tongue plunging into her mouth as their bodies slammed repeatedly against each other.

Her body tightened into itself in waves. Growing tension taunted her. She gripped Jake's narrow hips, her own lifting, bucking, urgently seeking fulfillment. The tension within her grew even more pronounced. She thought she would die from it. But she didn't.

Jake lifted his head and watched her shatter beneath him. Her mindless cry, the sharp sting of her fingernails in his skin, and the clutching convulsions of her lower body shoved him beyond the brink. A hoarse sound burst from deep inside him as he exploded inside her trembling body.

He eventually sank into the soft comfort of her body, his labored breathing like a fierce mountain wind, his heart thudding wildly, and his flesh so hot that Libby felt scorched by it.

Aftershocks suddenly rolled through her, prompting tiny interior tremors that stimulated rather than drained her. She clutched Jake's shoulders, surprise making her moan softly as he willingly stoked this new fire within her with gentle thrusts and a consuming kiss.

Jake released her mouth and lifted his upper

body. Resting his weight on his elbows, he cradled her head between his hands. "Go with it, love. Trust me and trust your body. Just go with it, Libby."

Her eyes wide and her breath coming in short gasps, she gave herself over to the passion and intensity gleaming in Jake's dark eyes and matched his deep thrusts into her body. Arching up against him, she felt her nipples instantly respond to the stimulation of the warm, damp hair of his chest. The coiling tension within her abdomen coiled even more tightly. Panting, she buried her face in Jake's neck just as her body erupted into yet another shattering burst of spasms.

Limp and drained, she collapsed against the pillows. Damp with perspiration, her body quivered with faint tremors as passion ebbed and she slowly regained her awareness of the world around her. Tears seeped from her closed eyes.

Alarmed, Jake rolled their bodies to one side. He stroked her slender back, trying to soothe her. After several quiet minutes he urged, "Talk to me, Libby."

She exhaled softly. "I feel so many things right now, and yet I don't know what to say."

He eased back and studied her face. "Are you all right?"

"I'll never be the same again."

A chill wind swept across Jake's heart. "Why not?" he asked quietly.

She shook her head, still stunned by what they had just shared. "I've changed."

"Is that why you're crying?"

She frowned and really looked at Jake. She saw

worry in his beautiful gray eyes and sensed that she had somehow caused it. Reaching up, she pressed her hand to the side of his face. He turned his head and dropped a light kiss into her palm. Her skin tingled, and she smiled despite the tears welling in her eyes again.

"I'm crying because I'm happy. I feel more complete than I've ever felt in my entire life."

He grinned at her soggy voice and her innocent candor. "What you are, love, is *completely* mine. Every beautiful inch of you is mine, and I don't plan to share you."

Amazed, she kept silent. She knew that the reality of the outside world would eventually destroy the possessive note in Jake's voice, but she wanted to savor his words for now. She also wanted to believe that he really meant them, but she knew deep in her heart that she couldn't afford the risk of actually believing bedroom talk.

Jake pulled her into a snug embrace, his arms fiercely possessive as he held her. "Woman, you made me ten years older with your crying. I thought I'd hurt you."

Libby laughed through her tears and returned his tight hug. She then carried her newly discovered courage a step forward and gave herself permission for the second time that evening to bask in Jake's warmth and sensuality, but only for the duration of his stay at Hancock College. Anything more, she realized, would be impossible.

Libby drifted to the edge of wakefulness in the hour just before dawn when she felt something warm and wet trailing up and down her spine. The sensation of being licked by delicate tongues of flame soon nudged her into complete awareness.

Jake smoothed her long hair aside and found her nape with his lips. Sprawled on her stomach with her legs apart and her face buried in a pillow, Libby shivered and then moaned softly when she felt his warm hands steal beneath her body and clasp her breasts.

"Feels good," she whispered, her voice sleepy and sexy to Jake's ears.

"*You* feel good."

Crouched over her, Jake continued to leisurely explore the satiny-smooth skin of her neck with his lips and tongue while he also teased her nipples into tiny dagger-points of desire with his fingers.

Her flesh tingled, and her hips, lifted of their own volition. Her stomach muscles clenched when she felt one of Jake's hands glide beneath her torso as he shifted over her body.

The circular motion of his hand at the base of her abdomen, in concert with the fingers of his other hand moving back and forth between her tender breasts, sent wave after wave of desire crashing over her. She trembled and throbbed and ached everywhere, her body readying itself for his possession even as she craved the same tactile freedom he now enjoyed.

"Let me touch you too," she murmured greedily.

He reared up, a possessive hand skimming down her spine as he lifted his weight from her hips. "Trust me, my love."

"You know I do."

Kneeling between her spread legs, Jake clasped her hips, lifted them up a few inches, and teased her receptive flesh with his arousal. He couldn't take his eyes off her—exposed, beautifully vulnerable, and innately sensual. He watched the provocative undulation of her body with no small amount of awe as she answered each teasing foray. He had the fleeting thought that he might have finally discovered the real Libby Kincaid.

Libby suddenly surged back against him, a thoroughly willing accomplice to Jake's predawn passion. He ground his teeth together as she impaled herself on him. He tried to hold her perfectly still, but her body consumed him. The delicate muscles now sheathing him trembled and tightened convulsively and brought an answering shudder from his entire frame.

His control dissolving, Jake sucked in a lungful of air and caught her hips in order to slow their movement. "You're trying to devour me, aren't you, my love? I want to make this last for you. We've got all the time in the world, you know."

She exhaled heavily and contradicted him. "My body doesn't feel like it's got any time at all."

"That's what your body's telling mine too," he conceded through clenched teeth.

Beads of sweat dotted his forehead, and his muscular thighs vibrated with tension as he remained kneeling behind her. He set their pace, though, a slow, determined, rhythmic blending of slick, hot flesh that obliterated control and threatened sanity.

Libby completely abandoned herself to Jake's dominance. She breathed deeply, lost in the tension escalating within her. When she finally opened her eyes, she saw the reflection of their joined bodies in the mirror. Her heart momentarily stilled in her chest and then started to beat like an overwound child's toy. She clutched at the rumpled bedding beneath her fingers, the erotic visual image of two naked bodies aligned to form one assaulting her senses and shredding her nerves.

"Jake!"

He felt the abrupt change in her, and he recognized the unique kind of sensual urgency that overpowered reason, destroyed good intentions, and transformed Libby into a wildly wanton creature in the blink of an eye. Quickening his pace, Jake responded to her need by thrusting deeply enough to touch her soul as he purposefully stroked the dark silk between her legs with his fingertips.

Libby screamed at the zenith of her climax, but her hips continued to move in an almost frenzied manner.

Jake's control instantly evaporated. He repeatedly surged against her in a quest for completion. With his head thrown back and his body burning with tension, he quickly reached the point of no return and then thrust deeply into her one final time. The sharp twisting of her hips triggered an explosion that sent him crashing into oblivion.

They couldn't speak.

Neither tried.

Still embedded in her body, Jake slumped forward across her hips and back. Sprawled facedown on the bed, she welcomed his weight and the knowledge that they had found pleasure together. They held each other while the strong aftershocks of their lovemaking slowly subsided. They fell asleep a short while later, positioned spoonlike on their sides in the center of the bed with a quilt covering their still-joined bodies.

Eight

Jake slept soundly through Libby's quiet departure from bed, the hot shower she indulged in, and the sound of the hand-held dryer she used on her hair in the hallway bathroom. After putting on a Chinese-red caftan and leaving her newly washed hair unbound, she went into the kitchen, where she prepared a carafe of coffee, filled a bowl with an assortment of fresh fruit slices, and assembled mugs and napkins on a tray.

As she made her way down the hallway to her bedroom, Libby whispered a fervent prayer that the morning-after etiquette she'd read about in novels and seen in movies was accurate.

Hesitating in the doorway of her bedroom, her gaze immediately went to Jake. He was still sprawled in the center of her bed, the quilt they had shared during the night covering the lower half of his powerful body.

She smiled suddenly, a surge of awareness stirring deep within her at the very sight of him. A tremor of possessiveness flared to life in her heart, but she countered the flagrant emotion with a stern reminder that Jake wasn't destined to become a permanent fixture in her life. They were just too different.

Despite that, Libby exhaled softly, her attention shifting to the subtle achiness of her own body. Having discovered a new self and a new world in Jake's arms, she now realized that her only other intimate experience many years ago had been fraught with genuine fear and numerous emotional barriers. No wonder she'd hated it!

Libby almost moaned with distress when Jake opened his eyes. She needed time to compose herself and her thoughts, but he invariably denied her that luxury. His sharp-eyed expression told her that he'd been awake for quite a while. The dark bristle covering his cheeks and chin explained the beard burns on some unexpected spots of her anatomy, and the rakish smile he gave her sent her pulse hammering out of control.

"Morning," he said, his voice low and throaty and so sexy that chill bumps streaked up her spine.

"Hi. I thought you might like some coffee."

He rubbed his cheek as he hiked himself up against the headboard, his gaze on her slightly abraded chin and swollen lower lip. The quilt slid down to his narrow hips, the dark hair of his broad chest and flat abdomen an invitation Libby tried to ignore.

She lowered the tray to the nightstand beside the bed. She froze when Jake reached out, swept back the curtain of dark hair concealing her face, and then ran a finger across the reddened skin of her mouth and chin.

"I should've shaved last night."

Libby paled, the splotch of color on her chin becoming more pronounced. "That's all right." She noticed his speculative gaze and busied herself with pouring their coffee.

"You looked very happy until just a second ago," he noted quietly. "Morning-after nerves, love?"

She straightened, started to move away from him, and then thought better of her juvenile behavior. "I don't know the rules for the morning after."

Jake's expression gentled at her admission. "You're an honest woman, Libby, so I'll be equally honest. I tired long ago of jaded social butterflies who treated lovemaking like a trip to the local deli. For the record, there aren't any rules. What happens between us is up to us. No one else has a say, and no one else has the right to judge."

When Jake reached out for her, she let him tug her down to a seated position at the edge of the bed. She slanted a hesitant smile in his direction. "I thought coffee might be a good place to start, since I wasn't sure what to do or say."

"Coffee's a good start," he agreed, his arms snaking out to encircle her waist. He grinned at her, a suggestive little grin that singed Libby's skin when she saw it. "But you're a better one." He drew her backward so that she wound up half reclining against his chest.

She felt Jake thread his fingers through her hair. She didn't quite understand his fascination with it, but she liked his hands on her, so she didn't complain.

"You're very experienced with women, aren't you, Jake?"

"Moderately."

Libby laced her fingers together in her lap, scooted even closer to him, and closed her eyes on a sigh. "Who's Carol?" She felt his fingers momentarily still in her hair, then start moving again.

"She's my executive assistant."

"And?"

"She's my very pregnant executive assistant," he clarified.

"Married?" She tried to make the question sound very casual. Her attempt failed.

"If you knew Carol, you wouldn't ask a question like that. Her parents are both ministers."

"You know her husband, then?"

He quelled the laughter trying to push past his throat. "Tom's one of my closest friends and a business partner, Libby. I introduced them, I was best man at their wedding five years ago, and I'll be godfather to their son when he's born."

She briefly despaired over the extensive surgery that would be required to extract her foot from her mouth. "I'm glad you have such nice friends."

She knew her comment sounded feeble, but she wasn't about to admit how dumb she felt or apologize for asking questions. Didn't her peers always tell their students that there were no foolish questions, just foolish people? She promised herself that she'd never make such an asinine comment to a student ever again. There *were* foolish questions. She'd just proven it!

Jake hugged her tight against him with one arm and continued running his fingers through the dense silk of her hair. "They'd like you, and I think you'd enjoy them." When she said nothing, he noted, "Jealous, huh?"

"Just curious," she corrected in her primmest tone of voice, but she spoiled the effect when she began to shake with laughter.

Jake joined her, the sound of his humor warm and seductive to Libby's ears. She lounged against him, so content that she knew she could easily start purring at any moment.

Lost in the comfort and serenity of the morning, they watched the shafts of sunlight creeping along the floor at the side of the bed. Libby dozed while Jake played with her hair. The security she felt in his embrace and the pervasive need to make their time together last as long as possible pushed back thoughts of the work she had yet to do on her textbook.

Libby jerked awake when the phone rang. She fumbled for the receiver, determined to put a stop to the shrill sound as quickly as possible.

"Yes?" she answered. It was Avery.

She absently watched Jake reach for an orange slice from the bowl on the tray she'd prepared. He took a bite from it and then popped the other half of the section into Libby's mouth as she listened to the department chairman drone on.

"All right, Avery. I'll be there in forty-five minutes." She paused and smiled at Jake. "What? No, I'm sorry. I can't get there any sooner." Libby's irritation with her boss quickly replaced her contentedness. "Good-bye."

She replaced the phone, reluctantly eased free of Jake, and got to her feet.

"Work?" he asked as he swung his long legs over the side of the bed.

She nodded, her gaze captured by the powerful flex and flow of his muscled body. "Department staff meeting. There must be a problem, because Avery is absolutely religious about his Saturday morning squash games with Dean Cassidy."

Jake pulled Libby between his sturdy thighs. He easily freed the three large buttons holding the front of her caftan together. She simply watched him, her expression bemused until he brushed the fabric aside so that it framed her full breasts and the silky dark curls at the base of her abdomen. Sucking in enough air to fill her lungs, she held her breath expectantly.

Looking up at Libby, Jake slowly and deliberately cupped her breasts in his hands and then flicked his thumbs back and forth across her nipples. They stood at attention like tiny soldiers of passion.

Libby moaned, the air scorching her lungs finally escaping. She felt a rushing sensation of warmth low in her belly, and her knees threatened to buckle.

"I don't want you to forget about me this morning," he murmured.

"Not possible," she whispered on a broken breath. "Not possible at all."

"Avery Mendenhall owes us an apology."

She clutched at his shoulders to keep her balance. "Avery who?"

Jake watched her expressive face, savoring the

intensity and immediacy of her response to his tender manipulation of her sensitive flesh. She reminded him of a smoldering stick of dynamite, and he wondered how she'd managed to conceal and suppress her innate sensuality for so long.

She smoothed his cheek with shaking fingertips as he circled her nipple with the tip of his tongue. Breathless moments later she mustered the courage to express her desire for him when she guided one of his hands down her torso and then tucked it between her upper thighs.

Jake willingly cradled the throbbing, wet heat of her body.

"Feel what you do to me," she groaned. "Feel how fast it happens. I don't think I know myself anymore."

He shuddered violently, his own body responding with hungry force to her words and her actions. He held her snugly, two fingers repeatedly dipping into the delicate folds of her body.

Libby began to rock and thrust against his hand. Jake stoked the fire blazing inside her until she lost control, found her release with a startled cry, and then began to crumple over him. He caught her before she collapsed.

"I can't believe the boldness you inspire in me," she whispered in a voice that fully displayed her shock at her own actions.

He smiled past the tension in his own body. "We've discovered the real you, Libby. I promised you this would happen. Didn't you believe me?"

"I don't know if I like being *discovered*." She straightened, drew back, and studied the self-satisfied expression on his face. She didn't know if she liked that either.

Her gaze traveled down his body, her eyes widening when she spotted the jutting reminder of their somewhat one-sided encounter. She looked up to his rugged face and noted his lazy smile and desire glimmering in his gray eyes. "You haven't . . ." she began awkwardly.

His smile broadened to a blinding display of even white teeth. He planted a searing kiss in the valley between her breasts before he got to his feet. "I will," he promised. "But not now. You've got a meeting, and I need to get back to the hotel and arrange that press conference."

Libby dragged her eyes from his seductive expression. She suddenly felt a wave of uneasiness roll over her. Jerking her caftan closed, she turned, seized a hairbrush from the mirrored tray atop her bureau, and roughly dragged it through her hair.

Jake understood the sudden shift in her body language, but he didn't criticize Libby for her mixed emotions. He had some of his own.

Instead, he stopped her hand, took the hairbrush, and replaced her angry strokes with gentler ones. "You're going to end up bald if you keep that up." He brushed her hair with long, sweeping strokes until he felt some of the tension ebb from her body. "I'd like to devote an entire day to doing this. I know I'd die a happy man."

Libby turned, her expression filled with uncertainty. "Why are we doing all this, Jake?" she whispered, the wrenching fear of potential abandonment gathering deep inside her.

Jake paused and considered her query. "Don't ask questions when you aren't ready to hear the answers, Libby. It's not a good idea." With that oblique remark, he handed her the hairbrush, dropped a kiss on her swollen lips, and strolled into the bathroom adjoining her bedroom. "You're going to be late, Professor," he called back to her. "I'll let myself out and lock up."

Libby sat at the end of a long table in a crowded conference room in the administration building that Avery Mendenhall had commandeered for his impromptu staff meeting. Despite her preoccupation with the night she'd just shared with Jake, she still heard with growing dismay the department chairman's description of the additions he wanted to propose for Jake's already overloaded schedule during his stay at Hancock College.

Several of her colleagues noisily vied for inclusion in the anticipated expansion of Jake's lecture schedule. A lengthy discussion erupted as they debated which undergraduate classes would benefit most from Jake's expertise.

Libby abruptly stood up. Her purse and satchel tumbled out of her lap and landed with a thud at her feet, but she hardly noticed the startled glances of the people seated around her.

The voices of those competing for Avery's attention dwindled slowly as they noticed that the department chairman's attention seemed riveted on Libby. She stood her ground, despite Avery's frown and the gnawing distaste she felt at drawing attention to herself.

She knew her responsibilities as Jake's liaison person, and she felt compelled to meet them. That she also might be protecting future time alone with him occurred to her, too, but she mentally sidestepped the realization for the time being.

Libby waited until the room was completely silent. "You can't mean to do this, Avery. Jake Stratton isn't a puppet. He won't permit us to yank his strings whenever it suits us."

The department chairman waved a dismissive hand in her direction. "He's a most accommodating man, Libby. He certainly won't object to an efficient utilization of his time. This meeting is being conducted to ascertain the most beneficial manner of putting his knowledge to work for our students. It is not, however," he chastised, "a debate on whether or not we are imposing on Mr. Stratton's generosity. Which, as far as I can tell, we are not."

Libby refused to back down. Ignoring the speculative looks on the faces of several people in the room, she said, with a firmness few in the room had ever heard from her before, "I don't agree with you, Avery. He's already bending over backward to accommodate a schedule that would test the stamina of a mule and try the patience of a saint. It would be unfair to impose on him any further, especially if we want him to return to Hancock in the future. Please don't forget that he's still responsible for his national and international business interests, as well as being on call to the White House and the State Department. As a witness to all those outside interruptions, I know that Mr. Stratton's barely had time to catch his breath since the welcome party at Dean Cassidy's home."

She ducked down, grabbed her satchel, pawed through it, and finally produced Jake's agenda. Shoving her braid back over her shoulder, she slid the folder down the center of the table like a bowling ball. It stopped halfway down the long oak table. Someone gasped. Avery glared at the file folder, and then at Libby.

Behaving with uncharacteristic stubbornness, she requested, "Someone pass that to Avery, please."

To the shocked department chairman, Libby said, "If you study Mr. Stratton's agenda, you'll see that there's virtually no free time in it, aside from the hours scheduled for lecture-material preparation. If previously confirmed arrangements are canceled, the fallout will be a disaster. And if we add anything else to his agenda, he won't even have time for meals."

"Perhaps someone else would be better suited for this assignment," Avery noted stiffly.

Libby noticed several heads bobbing in agreement. She paled, but she forged ahead, her tone matter-of-fact. "That's up to you, of course. Until that happens, however, it's my job as Mr. Stratton's liaison to preserve the integrity of the schedule he agreed to as a visiting lecturer."

She slowly unclenched her aching hands and pressed them to her sides as she glanced around the room. She saw surprise and dismay, but not a speck of support.

Libby's voice gentled, but she didn't realize it.

"I've watched him cope with performance pressure all week, and I promise you the man has a limit to what he'll tolerate. So far he's been patient, but I personally don't think we want to jeopardize his willingness to complete this grad-level lecture series."

She sat down as abruptly as she'd stood, her face flushed and her heart pounding hard. She refused to meet the eyes of those staring at her. She also refused to acknowledge the department chairman's blustery defense of his own grandiose plans.

Avery finally, and very grudgingly, agreed that the issue should be tabled pending further consideration. Libby breathed a sigh of relief, ignored the accusatory looks on the faces of her colleagues, and fled the conference room.

She was still shaking as she walked into her office ten minutes later. When she noticed the blinking message light on her phone recorder, she flipped the playback switch, sank into her chair, and heard the sensual voice of the one man who had the power to titillate her senses beyond redemption.

Pleased by Jake's invitation to join him following her staff meeting, Libby drove to his hotel once she regained her composure. That she had confronted Avery Mendenhall so instinctively and so publicly still amazed her, but then she'd already surprised herself several times during the previous week, she realized wryly.

She paused at the concierge's desk in the lobby for directions to Jake's press conference. Her sweatpants, Hancock College sweatshirt, and the plump braid trailing down her spine earned her a look of curiosity from the formally dressed man, but she ignored his inspection of her attire and thanked him for his help. Slipping quietly into the crowded pressroom, she found an empty chair in the back row and settled into it without drawing the notice of the media people vying for Jake's attention.

Television reporters with their camera crews, print journalists, and a few sleazy-looking characters who reminded her of the photographer who had burst into her living room the previous night were jammed into the modest-sized room. Libby noticed that at least a dozen microphones were taped together and positioned atop the podium.

Jake stood at the podium, his demeanor and attire casual as he fielded a wide variety of questions lobbed at him by the press. Libby felt a surge of pride as she watched him, but she quickly quelled the emotion with a harsh reminder that Jake Stratton was just passing through her life.

Although she tried to pay attention to his remarks on several international economic issues, the current fluctuation in the stock market, and the critical success of a film he'd recently backed, her thoughts strayed to the passion they had shared and the breathless wonder of self-discovery that lingered within her.

Libby could almost feel his hands on her body as her emotions and her mind soared with remembered pleasure. But the uncertainty she'd experienced just before they'd gone their separate ways that morning also cast a faint shadow of worry over her happiness.

The sound of her name interrupted her mental

meandering. Libby straightened in her chair. The survival instincts she invariably trusted urged her to exit the noisy pressroom, but she remained trapped in her seat by her panic that someone had discovered the truth about her father and intended to use it against Jake.

Jake concealed his dismay with an easy smile. "I'm sorry, I didn't quite understand your question."

"What's your relationship with Professor Kincaid?" the reporter asked again.

"Professor Kincaid and I are working together, but I'm certain you already know that."

"There's a rumor you two were spotted together at her home, after working hours."

Jake shrugged, his body language and his expression projecting an image of casual indifference. "As I said, we're working together." He glanced around the room and nodded in the direction of another reporter. "Any more questions on that trade agreement with the French, Bob?"

"Someone supposedly has some pretty compromising shots of you two, Jake. Care to comment?"

Jake gave all the men in the room a classic you've-gotta-be-kidding-fellas look, but he made a quick decision to provide them with enough of the truth to ease their collective suspicion that he might be hiding something from them. It was a ploy he'd used effectively in the past, and he hoped it would work this time. Libby, he sensed, needed time to come to grips with the public nature of his life.

"You already know that Professor Kincaid is my liaison with the college, Bob. She handles my agenda. Very efficiently, I might add. I'm also benefiting from her classroom expertise as I put together portions of the lecture series. I try to accommodate her teaching schedule, so we do work some odd hours."

In response to the bored expression on Jake's face, the reporter apologetically conceded, "I've seen the lady, and she's obviously not your type, Jake, but I'd appreciate a straight confirmation or denial now that the issue of Professor Kincaid's been raised."

Jake simmered inside, but he intended to protect Libby come hell or high water. He was also confident that she would understand his tactics once he explained them to her.

Lounging against the podium, he drawled carelessly, "Are you *really* serious, Bob?"

Everyone laughed. A woman from the local TV station asked a question on an unrelated topic. Out of the corner of his eye Jake noted Libby's hasty but discreet exit. He concealed the relief he felt that she had opted to leave the pressroom and that no one seemed inclined to follow her, but her stricken expression still gave him pause.

Jake glanced at his watch. "Let's wrap this up, ladies and gentlemen. We've been at it for more than an hour, and I'm ready for a late lunch."

He answered two more questions as he left the podium. Pausing briefly in the center of the crowded room, he shook hands with a couple of New York—based reporters he'd known for several years before making his way to the door. With a final smile and a wave Jake departed the press-room, his long-legged stride carrying him into the main lobby of the hotel within a few seconds.

As he scanned the spacious area for some sign of Libby, Jake realized yet again that she'd reawakened his long-submerged craving for a life removed from the limelight.

He wanted a normal life, and he wanted her in it. He intended to have both.

All the challenges in the world, he now knew, could never compete with the sensitive, multifaceted, and very passionate woman he had discovered beneath a facade of pragmatic indifference. As he walked toward her, Jake vowed that he wouldn't leave Hancock College without Libby.

Nine

Libby stood near a bank of elevators on the opposite side of the lobby from the pressroom. With color spotting her cheeks and her eyes blazing a scorching blue, she questioned her own common sense as she watched Jake cross the hotel lobby. A more worldly woman, she decided, would have walked away and not looked back, but the fury she now felt demanded a release, perhaps even a target.

She ignored his broad grin as he came nearer. When Jake paused in front of her, she tightened her hold on her leather satchel and stabbed him with a look filled with contempt.

"How was your meeting?" he asked as he towered over her.

"Fine."

She stiffened and stepped back a pace when he reached out and smoothed an errant wisp of hair away from her cheek. She took some satisfaction from the fact that his smile faltered as he withdrew his hand.

"And your press conference?"

He chuckled, but he looked guarded and wary. "Those things are always best when they're over, but I think I've redirected the focus of their attention."

"I've got something to say to you."

"I've got a lot to say to you too." He glanced around the lobby and noticed the knots of curious people studying them. "Why don't we get out of here and find a more private spot? We don't need an audience."

"That won't be necessary."

"Libby, it's obvious you're upset by what you heard in the pressroom, but I said what I did for a very good reason."

"I'm sure you did," she agreed. The emotional turmoil she felt drilled gaping holes in her heart and tautened her nerves. Burgeoning tears began to sting her eyes and swell in the back of her throat.

Jake turned and pressed the button for the penthouse elevator. Looking back at her, he extended his hand. "Let's go upstairs and talk this out."

She ruthlessly squashed her impulse to let him draw her into the elevator that now stood open and waiting for them. The hurt simmering inside her still throbbed steadily.

"I came to let you know that I'll be busy for the rest of the weekend." She glanced at her watch and managed a superficially bright look when she returned her gaze to his face. "I really can't linger,

Jake. Lots of work to do. Why don't we touch base Monday morning?"

"Libby, I was trying to protect you. You don't know these people the way I do."

"I can protect myself," she hissed back at him. "I've been looking after myself since I was sixteen, and I've done a good job."

"Libby—"

She snapped, "Please do not interrupt me again."

Startled by her fury, he gave her his full attention.

"I am not some damn bird with a broken wing, Jake Stratton." Libby didn't miss the narrowing of his gray eyes or the tension evidenced by the muscle ticking in his jaw. She ignored both, her anger and her realization that she wouldn't ever be the right woman for him driving her forward.

"And while I'm not as worldly or as sophisticated as the rest of your women, I will not apologize for that little deficiency in my personality. Furthermore, I do not need, nor do I want, you or anyone else as a protector, a manager, a manipulator, a rescuer, or an orchestrator in my life." She took a deep breath before continuing in an intensely low voice. "Is that clear?"

He moved as swiftly as a striking predator. Seizing her by the arm, he hustled her into the elevator. The door whooshed shut.

Libby hugged her leather satchel to her chest, her skin flushed, her heart thudding so wildly that she felt every pulse point in her body. She glared at him, infuriated with herself that she hadn't expected this caveman-style solution to any resistance on her part.

She watched him flip a switch at the top of the control panel next to the closed doors, and she knew she was trapped in an elevator car that wasn't going to budge until Jake disengaged the "hold" button.

He turned slowly and faced her. "I do not consider you deficient, and I have no wish to manipulate you or to orchestrate the events of your life. I will, however, protect you from the press and from your own naiveté where these people are concerned."

"I don't need—"

"You do *need*, Libby. Everyone *needs*. You apparently believe you can slog your way through life without a single ally. It's pointless and unnecessary."

"There's every *need*," she insisted, using his word to make her point. "As the saying goes, Jake, we come into the world alone, and we depart the world alone. Some things never change."

Stark dismay flickered in his eyes. "You're wrong, Libby. Let me prove to you just how wrong you are."

"The same way you proved you could make me want you?" she demanded belligerently.

"Dammit!" he exploded. "I'm not trying to seduce you. I'm trying to help you. I've spent years learning how to handle the press. You cannot do it overnight." Air gusted out of him as he exhaled heavily. "I don't have what you'd consider a normal life. Surely you understand that I live in a fishbowl. That photographer last night was a perfect example."

"That was just plain ridiculous," she scoffed.

"*That* was an invasion of your privacy," he pointed out in an uncomprising tone normally reserved for the boardroom. "You were on the verge of calling the police. There are rules for dealing with the press. You need to learn them."

"Why would I even want to?" she asked, bewildered by and suspicious of his motives. "They'll disappear once you're gone, and my life will be just the way it was before you arrived." Bleak, boring, and lonely, she realized.

Stunned, he took a step toward her. She backed up. The wall of the elevator car stopped her. The vulnerable expression on her face stopped him.

He worked for calm. A long search ensued, but he finally found it. "I wouldn't hurt you for the world, Libby. I was trying to protect our privacy."

Or you're ashamed that you're sleeping with me, she thought, and you don't want anyone to know.

"What I said to that reporter sounded flip, but I did it purposely. I don't want them hammering on you or upsetting your life." He studied her intently, and then he extended his hand. "Trust me. I know what I'm doing."

She desperately wanted to believe him. And she wanted to trust him, just as she'd trusted him throughout the previous night. But the skittish woman who lived inside her, the woman whose heart had already been given, felt vulnerable.

"Are you sure you aren't embarrassed to have

people know that we . . ." She stopped abruptly, silently cursing her own insecurity.

He started to laugh. "You're kidding, right?" Certain that she couldn't mean what she'd just said, he tugged her into his arms after grabbing her satchel and tossing it onto the floor of the elevator.

He kissed her, a thorough kiss that seared her soul and took her emotions on a roller-coaster ride. When he released her, she looked utterly enchanted.

"Take a chance on me, Libby. I won't disappoint you."

She cocked her head to one side with great effort, deliberate and calculating in her inspection of him as she tried to act carefree and worldly. Jake suddenly smiled that rakish smile of his. She caved in completely and allowed him to trample down her common sense and her self-protective instincts, but only for the time being. She knew they were too well honed to disappear altogether.

Leaning into him, she lifted her arms, looped them around his neck like a lasso, and then tangled her fingers in his thick dark hair. Libby sighed softly and gave herself permission to accept the pleasure Jake offered now, aware that she would pay the inevitable penance after his departure.

"What's the verdict?" he asked while he brought their hips together and rubbed himself against her.

"I'll take a chance," she said breathlessly as heat

and desire inflamed her. "But only if you keep your promise."

He nibbled briefly on her lower lip. His mustache tickled her upper lip. "What promise is that?"

"In a word. Lunch." With laughter and delight dancing in her bright blue eyes, she watched him swoop down for another sampling of her lips.

Libby successfully concealed her inner turmoil as they shared a tasty lunch served by room service in Jake's penthouse suite. As they ate, she questioned him about his recent forays into the entertainment industry. Convinced that she had gotten beyond her distress of his handling of the press conference, Jake appreciated Libby's interest in his work and shared some of the lighter moments of his involvement with the Hollywood crowd.

Even after their waiter departed, they lingered at the table, which was situated next to a wall of windows that provided a panoramic view of the entire Hancock community and Lake Hancock.

Libby covered her wineglass with her hand when Jake lifted the nearly empty wine bottle from the ice bucket beside the table and gave her a questioning look. "No more for me," she said. "The computer awaits."

Jake leaned back in his chair, his expression and his body relaxed as he studied her over the rim of his glass. "You really love your work, don't you?"

She nodded. "It's my whole world."

He grinned, the dimpled grooves deepening on either side of his mouth. "Not completely, I hope."

She teased, "Fishing?"

"No, not really."

"Seriously, Jake, my career will always come first. Nothing can replace it."

"What about our relationship?" he asked, his voice quiet and his expression suddenly guarded.

"What about it? Are you asking me for a definition of what we've shared so far, or are you asking me where our relationship, if we can even call it that given how little time we've known one another, stands when measured against my professional goals?"

He considered her questions for several moments. Libby clasped her hands together in her lap as she watched him, aware that this was her chance to let him know, once and for all, that she could cope with the reality of an affair with the same cool indifference of his past lovers.

"Both, I guess," he finally answered.

"All right. Friends and lovers would be the most straightforward definition." She kept her eyes on his face, her expression quite earnest as she forced herself to lie. "As far as measuring my commitment to my career against my willingness to become entangled in the uncertainty inherent in any relationship, loving or otherwise, then the career takes precedence over everything and everyone else."

"That's very analytical of you."

She didn't miss the harsh tone that had crept into his voice. "Perhaps."

"You surprise me, Libby."

"Why?" she asked gently. "I'm being realistic. Surely you've been involved with several career-focused women over the years. None of what I've just said should come as a surprise to you, especially since you profess to believe in the equality of the sexes in the business world."

"Of course I do, but not at the expense of every shred of personal happiness."

"My career makes me very happy."

"But does it keep you warm at night?" he muttered.

She managed a faint smile, although her heart ached painfully. She couldn't help thinking of how cold and lonely her nights would be once he was gone.

Getting up from her chair, Libby walked around to his side of the table. She leaned down and pressed a light kiss to his lips. When she felt his fingers slide across the back of her neck, a shiver electrified her entire body. She whispered, "I thought you might like to do that for me."

"Count on it, love. Count on it," he cautioned in a dangerously low voice before he brought her down into his lap and seduced her mouth with deeply possessive thrusts of his tongue.

Libby surrendered to him, despite her profound regret that she'd been forced to withhold the truth of her real feelings.

Loving Jake, she realized, would have to remain a private emotion. Wanting Jake, she knew, would eventually lead to disappointment. That she loved and wanted him, in spite of the absence of any hope for a shared future, brought a frantic urgency to her response to him.

Jake surged to his feet and carried her into the bedroom. His harsh facial expression and the tension gripping his body telegraphed the intensity of his desire to Libby. Infused with equally intense emotions, she became clumsy as she struggled with the buttons of his shirt. Her mouth grew voracious as she tangled her tongue with his.

Stark passion for each other centered their world on the currents arcing between them as they shed their clothing. Tense moments of breathless anticipation constituted all the foreplay they could tolerate.

Jake loosened Libby's braid with sure fingers, his hands plunging into her hair as their bodies tumbled onto the bed. They merged hungrily, without pretense and without the necessity of a prelude.

She reached her precipice quickly. Jake deepened and sharpened his thrusts into the slick heat of her body. He drove her past the edge and into a climax that threatened her consciousness, but she continued to undulate beneath him, so much so that she destroyed his control with little effort. He followed her into a sensual abyss that pitched him headlong into a world of shattering pleasure and breathless release.

Several hours later, as he watched her dress from his slouched position against the headboard of his bed, Jake knew that he had no choice but to accept the challenge of proving to Libby that emotional commitment was both possible and necessary. He also knew he couldn't rush her, so he forced himself to trust instincts that urged patience on his part.

Nonetheless, the corporate genius with the soul of a master tactician consciously began to plot the evolution of a relationship that would result in

Libby committed to him. The mortal man whose heart now occupied a position of jeopardy refused to consider the possibility of failure.

"You're a bad influence, Jake Stratton."

He grinned at her and flung back the covers, arrogantly naked as he swung his long legs over the side of the bed and got to his feet. "Know any better way to spend the afternoon?" he asked as he took the hairbrush from her hand and repeatedly stroked it through her long tresses.

"Absolutely none," she admitted, her scalp tingling from the repeated brush strokes. "But I should be working."

"Braid?" he asked after handing her the brush.

Surprised, she said, "Please."

He concentrated on the task, and she watched him with the help of a nearby mirror. Libby silently marveled over the perfection of his muscular body, while simultaneously appreciating the masculine confidence of a man willing to take on the bothersome chore of braiding a woman's hair.

"You must've been a Boy Scout."

He said nothing as he placed the plump braid over her shoulder. Libby fastened a clip to the end of it, ignored the uneven weave, and flipped it back into position.

Before she could turn around, Jake tugged her back against his body. He studied their reflection for several quiet moments before he spoke. "No time for Scouts where I grew up. I was lucky I didn't end up in jail or dead in some back alley." He inhaled deeply, not really seeing the shock in her eyes. "My mother sometimes needed help when her arthritis bothered her. It helped her relax when I brushed her hair for her."

She saw the distant look in his eyes. "Most men wouldn't admit doing things like that."

He refocused on her face, his melancholy expression flitting quickly out of sight. "I'm not most men."

"No, you're not, are you?" she whispered, a frown marring her smooth forehead.

"Do you want me to be, Libby?" he asked intently. "Would it make it easier for you if I were like other men?"

Easier for what? she wondered. Uncomfortable with the shift in their conversation, she ducked out from under his loose hold. "I like you just the way you are, but I really need to get home."

Jake nodded, stepped into a pair of slacks, and then walked her to the elevator. "How about dinner?"

"How about a late visit?" she countered as she stood in the center of the penthouse elevator. "I'll have a snack while I'm at the computer." A thought occurred to her. "We should get to work on your lectures for next week too."

He stopped the closing door with the palm of his hand. "Tomorrow. Tonight we'll deal with your workaholic tendencies."

She smiled and wagged a finger at him when he released his hold on the doors. "Said the kettle to the pot!" She felt a certain satisfaction that she'd finally managed the last word in a discussion with Jake.

Jake rescued Libby from a five-hour stint at the computer shortly before midnight. After helping her into a heavy jacket, he hustled her out to the waiting warmth of his car.

Libby didn't protest his high-handed behavior, nor did she question their destination. She simply relaxed and let the tension drain from her body during their silent drive to the southern bluff overlooking Hancock Lake.

"The night fires!" she exclaimed when she noticed the blazing bonfires ringing the lake. "I'd completely forgotten about them this year."

"I noticed them from the penthouse a little while ago."

She glanced at him. "Did you remember the tradition?"

He shook his head. "Not really. My first impulse was to call the fire department, but the uniformity of the fires finally jogged my memory." He laughed. "I spent a lot of weekends as a student helping haul wood for those tepee-shaped bonfires."

"The kids seem to enjoy it. I guess it's safe to assume the Hancock football team was victorious today. Otherwise, the fraternities wouldn't have put a torch to the night fires."

He shifted in his seat and leaned against the door on his side of the car. "You like football?"

"Honestly?" At his nod she admitted, "I hate being deafened by screaming fans and having my toes turned into ice cubes. I do like the hot dogs at the stadium, however." She shrugged. "Sorry, but a fireplace and a good book sounds more rational, and supremely more comfortable, to me."

He leaned forward, the seduction glinting in his eyes evident despite the dark interior of the car.

She met him halfway, heat swarming through her bloodstream like a thousand fireflies.

"How about a good man, instead?"

She drew in a shaky breath and then sighed unevenly as she lost herself in the depths of his gray eyes. Moving closer, he teased her lower lip with the tip of his tongue before drawing her into a kiss that made her breathless.

Despite the heady feelings coursing through her, she teased, "I might like that."

He squeezed her fingers and settled back in his seat. "Right answer. I thought we could drive up to Chicago one of these weekends. I'll show you the right way to attend a football game while we're there."

"Chicago?" she repeated, not sure that she'd heard him correctly.

Jake, his gaze now on the fires burning in the distance, didn't see the amazement in Libby's eyes. "Sure."

She cleared her throat. "Sounds lovely."

"Avery Mendenhall called after you left," he said a short while later.

"I had a feeling he might."

"Thanks for running interference for me, Libby."

"Part of my job," she quipped. She glanced at him and saw his lazy smile, and she knew she hadn't fooled him at all. "It was the right thing to do, Jake. Avery doesn't always know when to put the brakes on his enthusiasm."

"You needn't be charitable. I've met a lot of men like Avery Mendenhall over the years. They tend to get a charge out of being a big fish in a small pond."

She laughed. "That wasn't a compliment, was it?"

"You have to ask?"

With her hand tucked in Jake's larger one, Libby savored the ease of their conversation, the cozy warmth of the car, and the sight of the night-fire flames licking the edge of the black sky. She couldn't remember ever being this content or comfortable with another human being.

They didn't leave the bluff until Jake heard the even sound of Libby's breathing and realized that she'd fallen asleep.

"I can walk," she protested sleepily a while later when he lifted her out of the car and carried her into the house.

Jake shushed her and made his way into her bedroom. He pulled back the bedcovers, stripped Libby of her clothing, and put her to bed. After locking up and turning out the lights, he slipped into bed beside her.

As he held her through the night, Jake discovered a deep well of emotional satisfaction in simply offering Libby the comfort and security of his embrace while she slept.

Ten

Libby started to feel as though she were a passenger aboard a rocket streaking into the heavens. The days zoomed by, and she found she had to consult her calendar each morning in order to figure out which classes she had that day.

She maintained an uneasy truce with her emotions where Jake was concerned. His generous nature and spontaneous affection seduced her, but still she held herself back.

Her feelings for him reverberated within her like a perpetual echo. She longed to give voice to the thrilling emotions he inspired at least a hundred times a day, but she refrained from actually saying the words when they threatened to tumble out of her mouth. Instead, she conveyed her love through her passionate response to his lovemaking.

Not once did Libby suspect that Jake was attempting to prove to her that he was worthy of her trust, her love, and a long-term commitment. And not once did she realize that he felt she was slowly but surely distancing herself from him each time she sidestepped a question about her past or about her dreams for the future.

Despite the fact that she used all the free time she could squeeze from her schedule, Libby fell farther and farther behind in her quest to complete the final edit of her textbook. The deadline loomed, and panic lodged like a lump of cement in the pit of her stomach.

Too stubborn to ask for an extension from her publisher, she nonetheless refused to give up a single moment with Jake, even if it meant going without sleep. She crammed a lifetime of living and loving into the days and nights they shared.

She started wearing sunglasses and using makeup to hide the smudges of fatigue beneath her eyes. She catnapped in her office on campus, often waking up suddenly and in such a disoriented state that she sometimes didn't know where she was. She also ignored her conscience when it told her she was behaving like a greedy child set free in a candy store.

Libby hated lying to Jake when he questioned her about her obvious tiredness and the silences she lapsed into in the middle of conversations. Frustrated by his mounting worry, she fretted silently about how to distract him from it, but she couldn't find a solution that she could live with.

Libby breathed a sigh of relief when, during their fourth week together, Jake flew to Chicago for a series of meetings that had been scheduled around his lectures. Prior to his departure, he urged her to catch up on her rest during his overnight trip.

Libby knew how she would spend the time, but she agreed to his request so that he wouldn't worry, and wished him a safe trip. The frown of concern etching his rugged features haunted her as she returned to the Hancock campus and asked a fellow professor to cover her afternoon classes.

She carried his concern home with her as she settled in at the computer and embarked on a marathon session that lasted far into the night. An hour or so before dawn, Libby moved to the dining-room table to proofread her manuscript.

It didn't take long before she rested her head on her crossed arms, closed her eyes on an exhausted sigh, and promptly fell asleep atop a stack of manuscript pages. Several hours later she jerked awake to the sound of Jake's angry voice, a stiff back and neck, and the realization that morning had arrived.

"Dammit to hell, Libby! What are you trying to do to yourself?"

Bleary-eyed, she peered up at him. "I couldn't sleep. Thought I'd work for a while," she managed to answer around a thick tongue.

"You're lying."

She stiffened. "I don't lie."

"Are you trying to kill yourself?" He reached down to grab her shoulders.

"I told you, I'm working." She wrenched free of his hand and put her chair between their bodies. "You're supposed to be in Chicago."

"Didn't think I'd catch you, did you?"

"Catch me? I told you, Jake. I couldn't sleep."

"You're still wearing the clothes you wore when you dropped me at the airport yesterday morning. You haven't been to bed at all, have you?" He seized her chin. "You should see yourself. Dark shadows under your eyes, no color in your face, hollow cheeks, and you're losing weight."

"If you wanted a beauty queen, you knocked on the wrong door," she snapped.

Anger darkened his eyes. With obvious effort he clamped down on his emotions. "Tell me why you're doing this to yourself. At least when I'm here, I know you sleep part of the night."

She flushed, thinking of all the times she'd waited for him to fall asleep so that she could spend a few hours at the computer.

"Libby, I'm not a fool. I know you get up once you think I've fallen asleep. Just tell me why this darned textbook is so bloody important."

She pulled free and glared at him. "It's my future."

His heart sank with the realization that she obviously didn't consider him a part of her future. "When's it due?" he asked.

She heaved a sigh. "Soon."

"How close are you?"

Her chin lifted. "Close enough."

He moved so quickly that she didn't have a prayer of escaping his hands. Gripping her slender shoulders once more, he held her still. "Let me hire a friend of mine to help you. She's a free-lance editor. That way, you might live long enough to see the damn thing in the campus bookstore."

She shook her head, the pride that had driven her steadily since childhood wavering but refusing to give in. "No. I don't need help. I can do this myself."

Jake flinched as though she'd smacked him across the face. He released her and put some space between them. "Do you think you'll ever really trust me, Libby?"

"I do trust you."

"Then why didn't you tell me about your deadline?" He raked a hand through his hair, his frustration evident. "Why won't you let me help you? Why won't you trust me with your secrets?"

"I'm not a charity case," she insisted fiercely. "You couldn't have done anything about it, anyway."

"You're wrong," he told her. "I could have understood. I could have helped, but you won't let anyone help, will you? You won't let anyone close enough to share the load with you." He sighed heavily. "Every time I think we've made a little progress, we backtrack ten paces."

She stared at him, bewildered and suddenly afraid. "I don't know what you mean." Her chin shook. Tears filled her eyes. She pressed her hands to her face and swallowed a sob.

Concern flared inside Jake. Watching her was like viewing a building that was about to collapse. "Libby?"

"I'm so tired," she whispered as she started to sway. "Much too tired for this conversation."

Jake grabbed her as her knees buckled. He drew her up into his arms, venting his worry with harsh words as he charged down the hallway and into the bedroom.

Hurriedly undressing her, he bundled her into a

heavy robe and then tucked her under three quilts to stop the shivers that were shaking her body. "Don't make a move."

She nodded, too stunned to do anything else as she watched him grab the phone and punch in a series of numbers.

"Avery Mendenhall," he barked. "Jake Stratton calling."

"My morning classes," she groaned as she struggled to get up.

He gave her a deadly look that forced her back down. "Shut up, Libby, and stay put. You look like an accident victim."

She sank into the pillows, muttering, "Bully."

Jake ignored her as he waited for the department chairman's secretary to get her boss on the line. "Avery? Libby Kincaid's down with the flu. She won't be in for the next few days, maybe even the rest of the week."

As she listened to Jake's hard-edged voice, she despaired over Avery's reaction to the call. The man had little or no tolerance for illness.

"No, you can't speak to her right now. She's sleeping. Can you have someone cover her classes? She worries about her students." He paused, his expression still stormy. "No need. I'll keep an eye on her, and I'll let you know when she's well enough to resume her classes."

He hung up after saying good-bye. Getting to his feet, he glared at her. "You brought this on yourself, so don't give me any crap about being a bully."

"All right," she said with unexpected meekness.

Jake dragged a wing chair to the side of the bed

and made himself comfortable. "Close your eyes and get some rest."

"You're behaving like a prison guard."

He shrugged. "So sue me. I happen to like watching you sleep. It's a novel experience."

"It's about as exciting as watching grass grow. I think you're nuts."

"No kidding," he said grimly. "I *know* I'm nuts."

She sighed heavily and closed her eyes, too weary to fight the world, or Jake, any longer. She slept soundly until he roused her late that afternoon for a checkup by a physician he'd summoned from Hancock Memorial Hospital.

The doctor informed her that she was exhausted—a real revelation, Libby thought grumpily—and needed rest. For the next four days she remained in bed, except for periodic forays into the bathroom when nature called or for leisurely soaks in a hot bubble bath. Jake either prepared nutritious meals for her or had them delivered.

Libby didn't fight the enforced bed rest. Fatigue and Jake's worry quelled her instinctive rebelliousness. As she regained her strength and her perspective, she pondered her dangerously obsessive behavior regarding her career goals, and she came to the conclusion that she owed herself more than a steady diet of work.

Avery Mendenhall telephoned, but Jake grabbed the phone out of her hand when she answered it and dealt with the department chairman himself. She noted with some satisfaction that Avery didn't call back again.

Jake introduced himself to Clarice and per-

suaded her to keep Libby company on those few
occasions when he needed to leave the house.
Libby, who normally enjoyed her levelheaded
friend, endured her neighbor as she extolled
Jake's virtues ad nauseum.

She paid close attention, however, when Clarice
spent one afternoon explaining the best way to
enhance her facial features with certain types of
cosmetics. Clarice then made some succinct sug-
gestions about what Libby should do with most of
her clothes. She grudgingly agreed that a bonfire
just might be useful, especially after glancing
through some of the fashion magazines Clarice left
on her nightstand.

The doctor dropped in Friday afternoon and
pronounced her fit enough to travel to Chicago for
the weekend, provided she behaved herself. Trans-
lation: regular meals, vitamins, and proper sleep.
After being housebound all week, Libby eagerly
agreed to his rules. Jake appeared satisfied, paid
the doctor's bill over Libby's protests, and then
wrote a second check to the good doctor's favorite
charity.

Libby felt her stomach take a dive as the helicopter touched down on the helo pad atop a high rise
at the edge of Lake Michigan. She unbuckled her
seat belt as Jake tapped their pilot on the shoulder
and shouted, "I'll be right back, Mark."

Luggage in hand, Jake guided Libby out of the
helicopter and steadied her against the harsh
wind washing across the rooftop. They descended
two flights of stairs, paused while Jake unlocked

double oak doors inset with leaded glass, and then entered his penthouse apartment.

Extravagant. It was the only word that came to mind as Libby took in the luxurious penthouse Jake called home. It was also a tribute to the enormous amount of money his decorator had spent on his behalf.

Jake deposited their luggage on a low bench just inside the living room, his gaze on Libby as she scanned the spacious living room and dining room. "I don't like leaving you alone, but these meetings are important."

She turned and faced him, her expression intent.

"Libby?" He moved toward her.

"Don't worry about me. I'll be fine. I need to do some editing, and then I thought I'd get in some shopping. Clarice gave me the names of a couple of her favorite stores."

He moved even closer and stroked the side of her face with his fingertips. "You don't like it here, do you?"

"It's not that I don't like it," she said, her eyes gentle as she studied his hard-featured face. "It's quite beautiful, Jake. It just doesn't feel like you."

"It's not much of a home." His expression grew somber as he looked down at her. "It's convenient, though, and I'm not around much."

"It must be wonderful for entertaining," she said in an effort to make up for her clumsiness with his feelings.

"You're the first person who's seen it since I moved in last summer."

She sighed. "Open mouth, insert foot. My specialty."

He leaned down and kissed her, a quick hot kiss that made her insides buzz. "I don't like it much, either. I'm more comfortable at your place." Taking her hand, he led her back to the front door. "The number for the limo people is by the kitchen phone. Call them when you're ready to go shopping. No cabs, okay?"

She smiled up at him. "I didn't know mother hens had mustaches."

"Imp." He lightly swatted her fanny. "You're not completely well yet.

"The doctor said otherwise." She nudged him out the front door. "Get going."

"I'll be back about five. Our dinner reservation is for seven. We'll bypass the cocktail party and just meet everyone at the restaurant."

She silenced him with a kiss and then watched him charge back up the stairs to the waiting helicopter.

Libby devoted a few hours to editing several textbook chapters before calling the limo service. Armed with Clarice's fashion advice and a mental image of the dress she wanted for her evening out on the town with Jake, she embarked on her first full-fledged shopping adventure courtesy of several boutiques situated along Chicago's Magnificent Mile.

The prices boggled her mind, but after years of conservative living she knew her checkbook could handle the dent she put in it as she made a variety of purchases.

She bathed and dressed with great care upon

returning to Jake's penthouse late that afternoon. She then watched the clock in the living room edge toward six-fifteen as she nervously paced the Aubusson carpet in front of the fireplace.

"All dressed up and no place to go," she mused aloud just as the front door burst open.

She whirled around, her gaze flying to the stunned look on Jake's face as he strode into the entryway. Her long hair flowed over her shoulders and streamed down her back to her narrow waist like a shawl of the finest silk and satin threads. She'd feathered a wispy trail of bangs across her forehead, and applied her makeup so that it heightened the drama of her large blue eyes, high cheekbones, and generous mouth.

Jake stopped dead in his tracks and absently dropped his briefcase on a nearby hall table. He watched Libby clasp her hands together, and he felt a tremor of shock ricochet through his senses. He also registered her uncertainty when he saw the hesitation in her smile.

She looked so exotic and sophisticated that he almost didn't recognize her, although he knew in intimate detail the voluptuous figure now caressed by the fitted emerald-green cocktail dress she wore.

He watched her untangle her slender fingers and press her hands to her sides. His chest ached when she drew air into her lungs, exhaled raggedly, and then walked toward him, her shapely legs encased in sheer black hosiery and her hips undulating beneath the skirt of her dress in a subtle invitation that seduced him on the spot.

"You're running late."

"And you're exquisite," he said.

She paused a few feet from him and smiled with a radiance Jake had never seen in her face before. "Thank you," she breathed, her apprehension departing.

Drawn to her like a magnet, Jake closed the space between them and smoothed his fingers across the tops of several tiny pearls stitched into the bodice of her dress. He heard her shocked gasp when he changed tactics and brought her nipples to life with horizontal sweeps of his open hands.

"I want to kiss you," he said, his eyes darkening as he spoke. "But if I do, we'll never make it out the front door."

She shivered, torn between the desire to shut out the world and the knowledge that his friends expected them. "How about a rain check?"

Jake heard the trembling promise in her voice. His hands closed gently over her full breasts, but only for a brief, torturous moment. "I plan to collect on it later."

"I hope so," she whispered, her heart thudding wildly beneath his hands.

They arrived at the Ambria Restaurant on time, and immediately drew the attention of nearly everyone in the place as they were escorted to a private dining room in the rear of the crowded restaurant. Jake clasped Libby's hand more tightly when he noticed the covetous looks on the faces of the men who spotted her. When he finally mastered the jealousy knifing through him, he introduced Libby to his friends.

"Where are Carol and her husband?" she asked once they were seated at a large oval dining table.

"The baby's due any day now."

She nodded, her attention drawn to the matronly woman seated beside her, who remarked, "I understand you're a teacher, Libby."

"Associate professor," Jake corrected with a proud smile that drew surprised glances from several people at the table.

"I gather you two have only recently met."

Jake took her hand and laced their fingers together before she could respond. "Libby's also acting as my liaison with the college."

She slipped her fingers free, patted the top of his hand like a patient parent, and singsonged, "And Libby even knows how to speak when she's spoken to."

Everyone laughed, including Jake. The look he gave his friends made it clear that he knew he'd finally met a woman able to hold her own with him.

Jake savored her obvious enjoyment of the evening. He also drew quiet pleasure from the graciousness of his friends as they welcomed her into their closely guarded inner circle.

As he sat back in his chair and watched Libby, Jake grew reflective as the evening came to a close. His friends, accustomed to his many moods, overlooked his subdued manner. Libby, however, didn't.

"I had a lovely time. Everyone was wonderful to me," she told him with a worried look as they shed their heavy coats and hung them up in the foyer closet once they returned to the penthouse.

Jake turned abruptly and pulled her into his

arms, his embrace fierce, possessive, even urgent, and his body already hard with desire.

She slipped her arms around his waist and held him tightly. "What's wrong? You've been so quiet the last few hours."

"Nothing's wrong." He leaned down and buried his face in the scented curve of her shoulder and neck, claiming her as his own with gentle teeth and lips.

Fire leapt to life inside her, making her weak and malleable, but she fought her own instinctive willingness to be overwhelmed and then swept away by his passion. "Jake?" She clasped his face between her hands and forced him to look at her. "Please. Talk to me. Did I do something wrong?"

"Make love to me," he countered roughly, only half hearing her final question and the hint of uncertainty couched within it. "I need you, Libby. I need you now."

Defenseless against such a declaration, she welcomed his mouth when it slanted greedily across her lips. His tongue plunged deep inside to taste and tease and incite.

He also found and began to loosen the buttons that started at her nape and trailed down her back. Driven by a burst of undeniable desire, she tugged his tuxedo jacket free and then worked on the studs of his dress shirt, her mouth still clinging, giving, and receiving until she thought she would go insane if she couldn't absorb him into her flesh.

They created a path to the bedroom with the litter of discarded clothing. Sprawled across the center of Jake's bed, with her long hair in disarray and her body vulnerable and exposed to his gaze, Libby wore only sheer black stockings that ended at the tops of her naked thighs.

Jake shuddered as he watched her open her arms wide in welcome. She was every erotic fantasy he'd ever had. She reminded him of the bright flames of the night fires they'd watched together, and she provoked a sensual fever in his blood that he didn't want cured.

Discarding his briefs, he sank down onto the bed beside her and gathered her against the heat and power of his body.

"Your skin's on fire," she whispered.

He rolled onto his back, pulling her with him as a harsh sound escaped his throat. She went with him eagerly, but she purposely wound up crouched over him, her hands on either side of his head and her hips perched over his lower body.

When he tried to tug her down and encase himself in the dark heat of her femininity, she resisted. "It's my turn," she cautioned. Leaning forward, she traced the contours of his face with her lips, pressing tender kisses to his hard features and breathing soft sighs of pleasure.

Jake submitted willingly, despite the pounding pressure in his loins each time her breasts swayed against his chest and her hips dipped enticingly to stroke his pulsing shaft. He dug his fingers into the bedding, gripping it tightly to keep from surging upward and burying himself in her flesh.

She nuzzled his neck with taunting swipes of her tongue as she sank her fingers into the dense hair of his chest. And then she glided with agonizing precision down his torso until it seemed that she was flowing over him like an erotic wave, spilling her essence and her love across his body and into his pores like the finest scented oil. Her long hair trailed behind her bent head and loving mouth in a sensuous lover's caress that took Jake by surprise.

He shuddered violently beneath her hands and lips. "Libby!"

She fed on the raw, primitive sound of his voice. She also smiled, satisfaction streaming out of her on a trembling sigh, and absently wondered if he could feel her joy.

She moved lower still. He grabbed her head with shaking hands, stopping her so that he could catch his breath. He wanted the torture of her loving, but he knew it would destroy his control.

"Trust me enough to let me love you, Jake," she begged as she tugged free and knelt between his legs.

"I do trust you," he groaned in response. "I just don't trust myself."

Her fingers when she touched him were gentle and curious and thoroughly devastating. Her mouth, however, delivered a blow to his senses that rocked his soul and lifted his hips right up off the bed.

In giving pleasure, Libby discovered that she became the recipient of even greater pleasure. In testing the boundary of Jake's physical tolerance, she tested and then surpassed her own.

She eventually gave him what they both craved when she shifted forward and straddled his hips. He surged up into her, marveling over the designed perfection of their joined bodies. Her interior heat seared his flesh. Her delicate muscles tensed and trembled around him, coaxing, testing, taunting, and finally offering the ultimate temptation.

Breathless, Libby leaned forward and trapped Jake's hands on either side of his head. She offered her mouth, which he hungrily took, her tongue stabbing past his lips and teeth in an erotic reproduction of the movement of their lower bodies. Her breasts, swollen and sensitive, swayed gently, her taut nipples teasing his chest as she met and answered the summoning force of his surging hips.

She mindlessly chanted his name over and over again as they assaulted each other with passion. He gripped her hips, searching for and finally finding the sole explosive point of confrontation that yielded mutual death and rebirth. She clutched his shoulders and lost herself in a wilderness of sensation and coiling pleasure.

Bathed in perspiration and crying out hoarsely, they simultaneously reached a prolonged, wholly agonizing peak of ecstasy that seemed to go on forever.

Pummeled by the aftershocks of her climax, Libby finally slumped down across Jake's chest, her senses shattered, her heartbeat roaring in her ears, and tears trailing down her cheeks.

Stunned and shaken, Jake held Libby close to his racing heart and knew with overwhelming certainty that she had permanently altered his perception of the landscape of the world he inhabited.

He also realized that the most difficult hurdle they faced still hadn't been confronted or dealt with.

Eleven

Did I do something wrong?

Jake recalled Libby's question at odd moments throughout the night and well into the next day, but he delayed bringing it up until Sunday evening. He knew she didn't realize that she'd provided him with the opening he needed to broach the subject of her past. And his own.

Following a lazy morning spent in Jake's arms and an afternoon spent cheering on the Chicago Bears from the well-heated owner's box at Soldier Field, Libby folded one of the new sweaters from her shopping spree and placed it in her suitcase. She then tucked an array of colorful lace undergarments into the nooks and crannies around the sweater.

She glanced at Jake, who stood on the opposite side of the bed. "I think I'm still going to have to lug some of these shopping bags home with us. I can't get everything into my suitcase."

He grinned at her as he finished zipping closed his garment bag. "Your undies certainly can't take up much space. There's not much to that stuff, is there?"

Libby laughed as she recalled his amazement when he'd searched for a flannel nightgown for her the previous week. Instead, he'd discovered three bureau drawers stuffed with scanty bits of lace, silk, and satin in a rainbow of colors.

"My secret vice. You found me out."

"You're full of surprises. I keep wondering what I'm going to discover next."

"Stick around. I might have a surprise or two left in me," she teased, but the sober expression that appeared on his face stilled the humor bubbling inside her.

He circled around the bed and took a seat on the edge of the mattress. Tugging her into his lap, he wrapped his arms around her. "I plan to, Libby, but you don't really believe me, do you?"

She swallowed the unexpected lump in her throat. "I just don't want you to make promises you won't be able to keep," she said quietly. "I don't have unrealistic expectations about us. I never have."

Jake quelled his frustration with her conviction that a future between them was impossible. He knew better, and he was determined to prove it to her.

"Why did you think you'd done something wrong last night?"

"I thought you'd forgotten that." Although surprised that he recalled her question, she saw no reason to be coy. "I don't have much experience with the rich and famous, Jake, but your friends were all very nice to me."

"They're nice people," he agreed.

"I don't have anything, other than you, of course, in common with them. We're worlds apart. I accept that, because I have no other choice. I . . . I don't fit in, Jake. I never will. That's reality."

"That's not reality," he said sharply. "That's just some barrier you've erected in your head. What we're talking about here boils down to diverse life experiences, not different core values, which we share even if you don't seem to realize it."

She paled visibly. "You don't know the kind of people I come from, Jake," she insisted. "Buying a pretty dress and looking as though I fit in with your friends last night won't ever change some very basic facts about my life."

"Are you saying you don't think you're good enough to share a meal with people who've worked hard and become successful?" he pressed. "You've done the exact same thing with your own life, so tell me how you can be so different."

She nervously smoothed back a lock of hair that had worked free of her French braid. "They were nice to me because they're your friends. They obviously care about you."

"You're dodging the real issue here. Do you honestly think they care enough about me to be *nice* to someone they don't like?"

"Maybe." She shrugged. "Probably."

"You couldn't be more wrong, Libby. First of all, they're not phonies. They're very real people who've worked hard and gotten ahead. Millie, the woman who sat beside you, managed a truck stop before she married Bernard. He graduated from reform school at seventeen and then opened a neighborhood hamburger stand, which he eventually parlayed into a successful nationwide restaurant chain. Rosella first crossed the border illegally when she was thirteen. She was deported twice, but she risked coming back because she was determined to overcome the poverty and disease of her native country. She met her husband while they were both serving in the army. He's now a consultant to the State Department, and she's made a name for herself as a graphic artist." He wanted to shake her when he saw her disbelief, but he gave her a hard look instead. "Close your mouth. I can see your molars."

Stung by his sarcasm, she snapped her mouth shut and struggled to free herself. Jake grabbed her, easily subduing her flailing arms and twisting body as he hauled her back down into his lap.

"Now that I think about it, do they measure up to *your* strict standards? Are they good enough, given what you know about them now, to be invited into your home?"

She instantly stopped fighting him. Alarmed that he could think her so narrow-minded, she began, "Jake—"

He cut her off. "I never knew my father, Libby. He abandoned my mother about a month before I was born. After she lost her job on an assembly line, she worked a street corner to keep a roof over our heads, but I still loved her. I was a favorite with the truancy board in my neighborhood, which was your basic slum. I also spent two years on probation for stealing food and medicine when my mother became too ill to work. She died of pneumonia in a hospital charity ward. A judge gave me a choice between enlisting in the marines and going to jail, so I joined the marines and went to night school whenever I could. Later, I went to Hancock. Then I started my own business, and the rest, as they say, is history."

"But you're so . . . smooth." When he grimaced, she amended her remark. "I meant to say that you're a sophisticated man of the world. The president asks you for advice, for heaven's sake. Women everywhere want to sleep with you. And you've got a parade of media people hanging on your every word. How in the world can I compete with that? I know my limitations, Jake. I'm not a total fool."

"Who asked you to compete with anyone?" he demanded. "I certainly didn't. Damnit, Libby, I'm just me. Like you, I work hard. Like you, I'm independent and determined. And like you, I've been lonely, but I didn't let that turn me into a coward or keep me from pursuing my dreams."

He studied her for a long moment. Although he'd shocked her, even made her vulnerable by revealing his own checkered past, he still urged, "Talk to me, Libby. You're keeping secrets from me, and there's no need."

She worried her lower lip with her front teeth, then exhaled raggedly. Jake felt the shudder that rippled through her. He turned, shoved their luggage onto the floor, and then drew her down with him onto the bed so that their bodies wound up closely aligned.

"I can feel all the hurt and the fear you've got trapped inside you, Libby. Do you have any comprehension of how helpless I feel when you hide yourself from me? Trust me," he urged. "Trust what you know about me, and trust the fact that I care about you. Take those walls down once and for all. If you don't, we haven't got a prayer."

"A prayer of what?" she cried. "Why can't you understand that I want to forget the past?"

"I know you do, love. I did too, but it's part of who I am, and I refuse to sidestep the truth despite the fact that people may find it distasteful." Wise enough to understand the impossibility of what Libby wanted, he embraced her even more tightly. "Neither one of us will ever forget the past, but we can share the load of what we've learned to live with."

"But why do you need to know?" she whispered against his neck. "It's so ugly. I'm ashamed of that part of my life." Emotion clogged her throat and kept her from continuing.

"Yeah, it's ugly," he agreed grimly. "But it's right there, on the surface, every time you hold back a part of yourself, Libby. It's making you afraid. It's forcing you to shut yourself off from the very people who want to be a part of your life." He shifted so that he could see her face. "Can you honestly tell me I'm wrong?"

"No," she sighed, burrowing against him and resting her head on his shoulder. Although she sensed Jake's sincerity, she wasn't eager to reexplore the personal hell she'd lived through and then dealt with in private counseling several years earlier. She feared, too, that he would think less of her, and she loathed the idea that the media people who pursued him with such a vengeance would use her past to embarrass him publicly.

"I think you love me, Libby, but part of loving is trusting me with more than your body when we make love."

She stiffened, shocked to learn that her feelings were so transparent. She was on the verge of denying the truth, but her heart refused to let her lie. "Yes, I care for you, Jake, but that doesn't change anything. It just makes the situation between us that much more complicated."

He drew back. "The only complication we have to deal with is how we handle the future."

She stubbornly shook her head. "You're wrong. I'd be a liability, and I won't allow what I feel for you to endanger you or your success."

Exhaling heavily, he gathered her against his body, but he didn't press her further. He simply held her and prayed that she'd find the courage he knew she possessed to open up about the past.

He understood her sensitivity about the less savory parts of her background. He often felt the same way, despite his fierce pride in a mother who did her best and was still looked down upon by most *decent* people.

Libby found comfort and strength in the steady pounding of Jake's heart and the safety of his arms. Although she realized she risked his disgust, and perhaps even his contempt, she finally gave in to his demands.

"My father was what's called a roustabout," she said, her faint voice reflecting her personal shame and the terror she'd endured as a child. "We traveled the rodeo circuit so that he could find work. He had a short temper and heavy fists, and I remember experiencing both all through my childhood. He broke my mother's heart, and then he destroyed her spirit. I watched him take her love and use it against her. I hated him, but Mama always insisted that she loved him. She was obsessed with him, and she rationalized his abuse by telling me that he was just making sure we understood right from wrong."

Libby felt a chill sweep over her, but she kept talking. "He always drank heavily, and she was too weak to stand up to him. I learned to say nothing unless I was spoken to, and I kept out of his way whenever possible. By the time I was five, I'd turned being invisible into an art. Even though he finally wore Mama down and convinced her to drink with him, he still didn't stop beating her. I'd hide in the broom closet, knowing each time that he might actually kill her, but I was too small and too afraid of what he might do to me if I confronted him."

"No wonder you're claustrophobic," he muttered, his love and admiration for her quiet strength growing steadily.

Libby shivered violently. "I can still see her on her knees at his feet, begging him to stop while he kicked her and pounded on her. I lost count of the hospital emergency rooms the police took us to once he wandered off in a drunken stupor and the neighbors became curious enough to find out if we were still alive."

"Libby—" he groaned in dismay.

She shook her head. "Don't say anything, Jake.

You wanted to hear this, so just listen. I'll only say it once."

She heard a heavy sigh escape him, and she sensed his withdrawal. Tears gathered in her eyes, but she blinked them back and continued to reveal the sordid details of her first sixteen years of living.

"I first heard the word 'alcoholic' when I was about seven. I know now that my parents were sick, but as a child all I really grasped was that they didn't care about anyone but themselves and a steady supply of the booze they guzzled."

A sob escaped her. She rolled free of Jake and sat beside him. She studied her hands, unwilling to see just yet the disgust she expected to find in his expression.

"They were mean, cruel drunks who didn't care about me, who forgot to feed me, who didn't send me to school on a regular basis, and who didn't talk to me or tell me they loved me or pay any attention to me if I got sick or hurt."

Jake fought the rage rising up inside him as he pulled himself up beside Libby. "I'm so sorry, love."

She shook her head. And when he tried to draw her into his arms, she stiffened and pulled away from him. She felt soiled by her past. "Don't be sorry for me, Jake. I don't want your pity. Just try to understand that I didn't experience anything even remotely similar to a real childhood. I don't have a normal frame of reference, just a fantasy I've build in my head about how it should have been."

"I did the same thing," he admitted, "although for different reasons."

She wiped the tears from her cheeks and let herself really look at Jake. She saw compassion in his eyes, but no censure. She desperately hoped that he might really comprehend the inequities in her life and understand why she loathed being reminded of the past.

"We existed in a state of perpetual filth. I lived in the squalor until I was old enough to do something about it, but even then I knew my efforts were useless, but I tried . . . I tried so hard." Her voice broke, and she clenched her slender hands into tight fists. "We traveled from one rodeo to another, and one bottle of booze to the next, in a broken-down old trailer that reminded me of a foul-smelling coffin."

Jake reached out and placed a gentle hand on her shoulder. "Stop now, Libby. You've said enough."

Caught up in her memories, she didn't even hear him. "I overheard my father promising my virginity to one of his drinking buddies in exchange for a bottle of cheap wine on my sixteenth birthday. In retrospect, I guess I was lucky he didn't do it any sooner. I stole ten dollars from my mother's purse. Then I ran, as far and as fast as I could go. I slept in bus stations and abandoned buildings, I hitched rides, and I begged for food. When people turned me away, I waited for restaurants to close at night so that I could go through the trash. Living like a vagrant for a couple of months taught me some very valuable lessons. I finally found a job as a live-in baby-sitter for a college professor and his wife. They gave me my first taste of stability and encouraged me to enroll in night school."

Libby studied her hands for several silent seconds. When she finally looked up at Jake, she glimpsed the anguish she felt reflected in his expression.

"The night I ran away, I swore I'd never be as weak or as trusting as my mother. I've kept that vow. No one, not even you, can make me break it." Suddenly exhausted, she sagged forward and rested her head in her hands.

Jake stroked her bowed head. "No one's asking you to be weak."

Libby looked up, oddly strengthened by his touch. "Do you want to hear the rest?"

Despite the risk inherent in revealing what he knew, Jake couldn't let her relive any more of the past, so he relieved her of the burden. "You mean the part about working one menial job after another while you went to school, graduating at the head of your class each time you received a degree, or the part about looking for your mother and then finding out that Mick Kincaid had killed her one night ten years ago in a drunken rage in some two-bit El Paso saloon?" he asked, the strain of keeping his fury with what her parents had done to her under control killing him by degrees.

She stared at him, unable to speak, barely able to draw air into her lungs.

"I've known about it all for several days," he admitted. "And I'm still here, aren't I?"

She nodded, too shocked to do anything else.

"And I obviously don't think less of you. If anything, I respect your strength and your courage."

He reached out and drew her trembling body into his arms. "The only thing that worries me now is whether or not you're going to keep running."

"My father is an evil man. I can't ever let down my guard where he's concerned."

"You can trust me when I tell you that you have nothing to worry about where he's concerned."

"He killed my mother, and I have no doubt that he'd try to hurt me if he found me. You don't know what he's like." She gripped his shoulders. "Please believe me, Jake. He would think nothing of hurting me, and you, if he thought he would gain something from it."

He frowned. "Let me see if I understand what you're saying. You're going to continue to let your fear of a cruel drunk orchestrate your entire life. You're actually going to give him that kind of power?"

"I don't want you hurt! I couldn't bear it if something happened to you because of me."

"Why?" he demanded harshly. "Tell me why."

"Because I love you."

He crushed her to him, relief temporarily robbing him of his ability to speak. "He's dead, Libby. He died almost six years ago."

Stunned, she went limp in his embrace. "I can't grieve for someone I hated. Does that make me a terrible person?"

He shook his head. "There's no reason for you to grieve for him."

"I thought I'd created the perfect world until I met you, Jake," she said, amazement in her voice at how foolish she'd been. "But all I really did was build a cage to hide in whenever I felt threatened."

"You've done so much more than that, Libby. Granted, you lost your innocence early in life, but you didn't lose your gentleness or your decency. Those qualities are still a part of you, and that's why my friends enjoyed you so much last night. And you won't ever be like your mother, no more than I'll be like my father. We've both made important choices, and we've backed those choices with honor and integrity. No one can do any more than that."

"I should be furious with you. You went behind my back."

"That's true, but I had no choice."

"How?"

"How did I find out?" He shrugged. "I called a friend. He did most of the legwork."

"A private investigator?"

"Yeah."

"He won't . . ." Her voice trailed off.

"He deals with confidential matters all the time. You have nothing to worry about, and you don't have anything to hide. You're a survivor, Libby. That's something to be proud of."

"I'm not angry," she said with some surprise. "If anything, I'm relieved that you know."

"I hoped you would be. Someone I trusted a long time ago forced me to do what I've just made you do. It changed my life."

"Why put yourself through something like this, Jake?"

He peered down at her tear-smudged face. "You don't know?"

"I . . . I don't know what to think," she admitted.

He shook his head, his expression rueful as he tugged her back into his arms and held her. "What am I going to do with you, Libby?"

"Love me back just a little," she said in a fragile voice that nearly broke his heart. "And be my friend after you've left and everything between us is just a memory."

"You're a smart, sexy, and loving woman, Libby Kincaid. You amaze and delight me. You make me feel alive, and I think you're as hungry for me as I am for you. But you can be amazingly dense some of the time."

"I am," she whispered. "Sexy and smart, I mean."

"You are," he confirmed. "But I also think you're wise enough to realize that I can't do this anymore."

The pain was as devastating as she'd expected. "I always knew it would end."

He looked at her, his expression grim. "I want and need more than a part-time love affair when it's convenient. Life's too short."

"You deserve more." We both do, she realized. She tired to scramble out of his arms, but he refused to release her.

"I love you. Why can't you love me back enough to want to share a life and home with me?" he asked, anger edging his voice despite his best efforts to keep his frustration under control. "No one can hurt us. No one can take anything from us that we aren't willing to give."

"Did you just say you love me?" Shock made her whisper the question.

"Dammit, yes," he barked.

She stared at him, desperate to believe that she

mattered that much to him. "If my past gets out, it wouldn't embarrass you?

"Stupid question. Ask another."

She smiled then, a smile overflowing with love and disbelief and hope. Jake knew he'd never seen anything more beautiful.

"Would you tell me again that you love me?"

"Excellent question. And yes, I love you more than my life. I love you more than anyone and anything in this world. Now do you believe me?"

"I was only trying to protect my feelings when I told you my career would always come first."

"I know that now, love, but I didn't at the time." He brought her up against his hard body. "Marry me."

She wrapped her arms around his neck and pressed wild little kisses all over his face. "When?" she asked.

"Right now."

She grinned and pushed him back onto the bed. Crouched over him, she questioned, "Right now?"

Jake pulled her down until she was sprawled across his chest. He then captured her mouth. Several minutes later he asked, "Would it be all right if we wait until tomorrow morning? I have a feeling that the fire you just started isn't going to be put out for quite a while."

She answered him with a seductive smile and a sizzling kiss.

THE EDITOR'S CORNER

LOVESWEPT sails into autumn with six marvelous romances featuring passionate, independent, and truly remarkable heroines. And you can be sure they each find the wonderful heroes they deserve. With temperatures starting to drop and daylight hours becoming shorter, there's no better time to cuddle up with a LOVESWEPT!

Leading our lineup for October is **IN ANNIE'S EYES** by Billie Green, LOVESWEPT #504. This emotionally powerful story is an example of the author's great skill in touching our hearts. Max Decatur was her first lover and her only love, and marrying him was Anne Seaton's dream come true. But in a moment of confusion and sorrow she left him, believing she stood in the way of his promising career. Now after eleven lonely years he's back in her life, and she's ready to face his anger and furious revenge. Max waited forever to hurt her, but seeing her again ignites long-buried desire. And suddenly nothing matters but rekindling the old flame of passion. . . . An absolute winner!

Linda Cajio comes up with the most unlikely couple—and plenty of laughter—in the utterly enchanting **NIGHT MUSIC**, LOVESWEPT #505. Hilary Rayburn can't turn down Devlin Kitteridge's scheme to bring her grandfather and his matchmaking grandmother together more than sixty years after a broken engagement—even if it means carrying on a charade as lovers. Dev and Hilary have nothing in common but their plan, yet she can't catch her breath when he draws her close and kisses her into sweet oblivion. Dev wants no part of this elegant social butterfly—until he succumbs to her sizzling warmth and vulnerable softness. You'll be thoroughly entertained as these two couples find their way to happy-ever-after.

Many of you might think of that wonderful song "Some Enchanted Evening" when you read the opening scenes of **TO GIVE A HEART WINGS** by Mary Kay McComas, LOVESWEPT #506. For it is across a crowded room that Colt McKinnon first spots Hannah Alexander, and right away he knows he must claim her. When he takes her hand to dance and feels her body cleave to his with electric satisfaction, this daredevil racer finally believes in love at first sight. But when the music stops Hannah escapes before he can discover her secret pain. How is she to know that he would track her down, determined to possess her and slay her dragons? There's no resisting Colt's strong arms and tender smile, and finally Hannah discovers how wonderful it is to fly on the wings of love.

A vacation in the Caribbean turns into an exciting and passionate adventure in **DATE WITH THE DEVIL** by Olivia Rupprecht, LOVESWEPT #507. When prim and proper Diedre Forsythe is marooned on an island in the Bermuda Triangle with only martial arts master Sterling Jakes for a companion, she thinks she's in trouble. She doesn't expect the thrill of Sterling's survival training or his spellbinding seduction. Finally she throws caution to the wind and surrenders to the risky promise of his intimate caress. He's a man of secrets and shadows, but he's also her destiny, her soulmate. If they're ever rescued from their paradise, would her newfound courage be strong enough to hold him? This is a riveting story written with great sensuality.

The latest from Lori Copeland, **MELANCHOLY BABY,** LOVE-SWEPT #508, will have you sighing for its handsome hell-raiser of a hero. Bud Huntington was the best-looking boy in high school, and the wildest—but now the reckless rebel is the local doctor, and the most gorgeous man Teal Anderson has seen. She wants him as much as ever—and Bud knows it! He understands just how to tease the cool redhead, to stoke the flames of her long-suppressed desire with kisses that demand a lifetime commitment. Teal shook off the dust of her small Missouri hometown for the excitement of a big city years ago, but circumstances forced her to return, and now in Bud's arms she knows she'll never be a melancholy baby again. You'll be enthralled with the way these two confront and solve their problems.

There can't be a more appropriate title than **DANGEROUS PROPOSITION** for Judy Gill's next LOVESWEPT, #509. It's bad enough that widow Liss Tremayne has to drive through a blizzard to get to the cattle ranch she's recently inherited, but she knows when she gets there she'll be sharing the place with a man who doesn't want her around. Still, Liss will dare anything to provide a good life for her two young sons. Kirk Allbright has his own reasons for wishing Liss hasn't invaded his sanctuary: the feminine scent of her hair, the silky feel of her skin, the sensual glow in her dark eyes—all are perilous to a cowboy who finds it hard to trust anyone. But the cold ache in their hearts melts as warm winter nights begin to work their magic. . . . You'll relish every moment in this touching love story.

FANFARE presents four truly spectacular books next month! Don't miss out on **RENDEZVOUS,** the new and fabulous historical novel by bestselling author Amanda Quick: **MIRACLE,** an unforgettable contemporary story of love and the collision of two worlds, from critically acclaimed Deborah Smith: **CIRCLE OF PEARLS,** a thrilling historical by immensely talented Rosalind Laker; and **FOREVER,** by Theresa Weir, a heart-grabbing contemporary romance.

Happy reading!

With warmest wishes,

Nita Taublib

Nita Taublib
Associate Publisher/LOVESWEPT
Publishing Associate/FANFARE

FANFARE SPECIAL OFFER

Be one of the first 100 people to collect 6 FANFARE logos (marked "special offer") and send them in with the completed coupon below. We'll send the first 50 people an autographed copy of Fayrene Preston's THE SWANSEA DESTINY, on sale in September! The second 50 people will receive an autographed copy of Deborah Smith's MIRACLE, on sale in October!

The FANFARE logos you need to collect are in the back of LOVESWEPT books #498 through #503. There is one FANFARE logo in the back of each book.

For a chance to receive an autographed copy of THE SWANSEA DESTINY or MIRACLE, fill in the coupon below (no photocopies or facsimiles allowed), cut it out and send it along with the 6 logos to:

FANFARE Special Offer
Department CK
Bantam Books
666 Fifth Avenue
New York, New York 10103

━ ━ ━ ━ ━ ━ ━ ━ ━ ━ ━ ━ ━ ━ ━ ━ ━ ━

Here's my coupon and my 6 logos! If I am one of the first 50 people whose coupon you receive, please send me an autographed copy of THE SWANSEA DESTINY. If I am one of the second 50 people whose coupon you receive, please send me an autographed copy of MIRACLE.

Name _____

Address _____

City/State/Zip _____

Offer open only to residents of the United States, Puerto Rico and Canada. Void where prohibited, taxed or restricted. Allow 6-8 weeks after receipt of coupon for delivery. Bantam Books is not responsible for lost, incomplete or misdirected coupons. If your coupon and logos are not among the first 100 received, we will not be able to send you an autographed copy of either MIRACLE or THE SWANSEA DESTINY. Offer expires September 30, 1991.

Bantam Books   SW 9 - 10/91   special offer
                                                     cut on dotted line

THE LATEST IN BOOKS
AND AUDIO CASSETTES

NEW!

Handsome Book Covers Specially Designed To Fit Loveswept Books

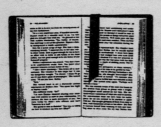

Our new French Calf Vinyl book covers come in a set of three great colors— royal blue, scarlet red and kachina green.

Each 7" × 9½" book cover has two deep vertical pockets, a handy sewn-in bookmark, and is soil and scratch resistant.

To order your set, use the form below.